—•••—

CHECKMATE

A Deadly Game of Cyber Espionage

—•••—

MARY JANE FORBES

Todd Book Publications

Checkmate
A Deadly Game of Cyber Espionage

ISBN: 978-0615954936 (sc)

Printed in the United States of America
Todd Book Publications
4th Edition: 10/2017
Port Orange Florida

Website: www.MaryJaneForbes.com
Author photo: Ami Ringeisen

Aztec II Necklace
Betty Parlette, Designer

This piece uses an embellished gemstone donut for the focal piece and a simple pattern of matching gemstone tubes and spacers for the rest of the necklace.

To embellish the gemstone donut, use a 24 or 26 gauge wire. Wrap around the donut several times. As you make each wrap, add small beads (or whatever complements the stone) and make small bends in the wire to keep the beads in place and to add interest.

To string the necklace, cut 24 inches of flexible beading wire. Make a bail to hold the donut by stringing size 11 seed beads in the center of the wire. Loop the wire through the hole of the donut. You can either make a lark's head knot or use a bead cap.

Then strand the matching gemstones and whatever spacers you choose on each side until your necklace is the desired length.

Attach clasp by adding a crimp tube, taking the wire through the clasp and back through the crimp, crimping with crimping pliers. Repeat on the other side. Make sure the beads are snug, no wire showing, but not too tight.

Courtesy of Imagine That!®

**Necklace that Brenda purchased at the grand opening
of the Cyber Café.**

—•••—

For Gordon, who introduced me to
personal computing many years ago.

—•••—

Acknowledgements

Thanks to the NSERB (North Side Editorial Review Board) Vera, Lorna, Jean, and Adele, as well as my daughter Molly, and Roger and Pat Grady for struggling through the initial draft.

The bead shop, Imagine That!®, where the House of Beads Mystery Series began. Carolyn and Scott—thank you for your continued support.

Thanks to my son, Rob, for his technical support.

—•••—

CHECKMATE is the third book in the House of Beads Mystery Series. Look for book four, IDENTITY THEFT, now available.

In the meantime, head for that comfy chair and enjoy the following pages. You will meet Brenda Kittles as she joins Catherine, Manny, Daytona Pete, Tillie, and Fred in their struggle to thwart the hacker.

—•••—

CHECKMATE

A Deadly Game of Cyber Espionage

—•••—

Prologue

— • • • —

MONDAY, 3 A.M.

A cloud drifted over the full moon, casting an eerie shadow on the earth below. Hot, humid, August air enveloped the east coast of Florida. Late night showers were predicted over Daytona Beach.

The street was void of traffic. Three customers, dressed in dark blue mechanic's overalls, their wet boots dripping on the floor, sat at a counter eating their breakfast in the all-night diner.

The diner's neon sign slowly blinked O P E N, one letter at a time, the yellow letters popping into the night air. Across the street the motel's sign flashed VACANCY. The beat of the two signs punctuated the darkness, the neon rhythmically dancing on the street's wet pavement.

The motel was dark. The rooms empty, or the occupants asleep. All, except for one room.

This room appeared dark from the street, but its window was raised a few inches. The dusty white curtain covering the window fluttered slightly in the occasional breeze. A cigarette butt glowed red. Then the glow turned black from lack of oxygen and was crushed against the bottom of the empty tuna fish can.

A single siren off in the distance suggested an emergency, someone in trouble. Inside the room, the only sound was the clickity-click of the keys as fingers tapped commands on the computer's keyboard. Images flashing across the screen of the laptop, abruptly ceasing when the fingers stopped tapping.

"Access Denied" displayed on the screen.

"Damn!"

Another barrage of clickity-clicks—images again swirling on the monitor.

"Access Denied."

"Okay, here's one you'll recognize." Clickity-clickity-click.

The computer screen refreshed. The computer's speakers came to life. "Good evening, Mr. Stone." A smirk crossed the face of the hacker.

Chapter 1

— • • • —

CLIMBING INTO THE SHUTTLE van with his staff, Russell Stone had to admit that his heart was beating a faster than normal. He dreamed of a day like this for his company as he toiled over the past year formulating his bid. He poured his heart and soul into the project. Then it happened. After a tough competition, his company won the coveted contract for the Daytona Beach Tower Project—a multiplex development on the ocean.

The van pulled away from the curb, heading beachside. Animated chatter from the staff grew along with their excitement during the short ride. The vehicle turned down the sandy, makeshift road to the ocean. It then swung south, traveling on the beach to where a group of people had gathered.

The day was perfect for the groundbreaking ceremony even though it was hot. There wasn't a cloud in the azure blue sky. The salty air was invigorating as the ocean waves gently lapped the shore. Each wave rode in with the sun's rays bouncing off the sparkling water, welcoming the van and its occupants.

Russell turned to his chief financial officer sitting next to him. "This is quite a moment, Vera. You've been with me since day one. I have to admit I've never been this excited about a project, a little nervous, too. This development is a huge undertaking."

"Russell, if anyone can pull this together and help catapult Daytona Beach into an even bigger tourist attraction, it's you," Vera said, giving his arm a supportive pat.

Russell walked to the front of the shuttle to address his team.

"It's been five months since Stone & Associates was awarded the honor of building a truly unique development on the shores of Daytona Beach, and today we officially break ground. I invite you to pick out a shovel from the box behind our driver. They're engraved with today's date, and Daytona Beach Tower Project. You may keep it as a souvenir. Bring your shovel, and your best smile. As you can see, reporters are on hand to capture the moment. So, let's go dig some dirt."

Chuck walked up to Stone greeting him with a hearty handshake. "Hi, boss," he said. "The big day has finally arrived."

"Looks like you have everything ready," Stone said, with a broad reciprocating smile.

"We're just waiting for you to give the word," Chuck replied, his eyes twinkling in anticipation.

"Okay, everyone, let's get this baby started," Stone said. He and his group made their way along a temporary boardwalk away from the sandy beach to a line of stanchions festooned with red, white, and blue ribbons fluttering softly in the warm ocean breeze. Russell greeted the Mayor and the President of the Chamber of Commerce, handing each a shovel.

The reporters started snapping their cameras, and Channels 13 and 9 focused their video equipment from their choppers overhead. Stone pushed his shovel into the ground, looked at his staff of seven and his guests, waving his hand for them to join him. Jamming their shovels into the ground, they looked up with broad smiles for the media.

Seemingly out of nowhere a caravan of cars, led by an unmarked green bus, pulled down the sandy road honking their horns. The entourage turned south and stopped. Eight cars pulled alongside the bus forming a line facing the area where the groundbreaking was taking place, about fifty yards away. The occupants of the bus and cars emerged from the vehicles. The apparent leader raised a bullhorn to her lips and shouted, "Hotel no. Public beach yes." There were more than sixty protestors flanking their leader. The gladiators, girded for battle, pulled out signs and started chanting for their rights to convenient beach access. "I pay taxes. I want access."

The media turned their cameras to the north to capture the action of the protestors. Just as the television channels started to send the live-feed to their stations an ear-splitting explosion was heard behind them. The cameras swiveled around, training their equipment to the south, down the beach about thirty yards where a large storage shed was ablaze. The choppers also swung around to catch the fiery flames shooting in the air. A newspaper reporter's camera was positioned in such a way that the burning shed was in the background of Stone's staff holding their shovels—a colorful picture for the front page of tomorrow's edition.

Sanchez yanked his cell out of his pants pocket and dialed 9-1-1, requesting the operator to dispatch the fire department. He and one of his foremen ran down the beach to the shed. Within minutes, a fire truck sped down the packed sand. The truck was blocked by the line of protestors, but the driver navigated the big engine into the surf and back onto the beach to get to the fire.

Firemen jumped off the rig and began pulling the hoses from their compartments. Using the trucks' water tanks, they opened the nozzles full force quickly dousing the flames. The shed was gutted, leaving charred items made from metal lying in the ashes, some gas cans, and small tools. The whole episode lasted a little over fifteen minutes.

For the most part, the protestors seemed as shaken as the spectators, but their leader did not appear to be shocked.

Stone joined Sanchez and the firemen by the leveled shed. Dying embers gave off a few puffs of smoke. Hissing could be heard where the water puddled.

"Chuck, what the hell do you think caused the shed to blow?" Stone yelled, over the noise from the fire truck's engine.

"I don't know, but you can be sure I'll find out."

"Don't let anyone near the shed and don't touch that gas can— looks like the culprit. Treat the area as a crime scene."

Chapter 2

— • • • —

THE SHUTTLE PULLED AWAY from the beach onto Route A1A heading back to Stone & Associates, a distinguished architectural and building company on Florida's east coast. Russell Stone, President, had scheduled a construction kickoff meeting over lunch following the groundbreaking ceremony.

The van turned into the company parking lot and was greeted with several police vehicles, red lights whirling.

"What the hell is this all about," Russell said, moving beside the van's driver, and peering through the windshield as the van came to a stop. Looking over his shoulder at his staff, he said, "Please go on in the building while I talk to the police. I'll let you know why they're here when we meet for lunch."

— • • • —

Entering the conference room, Catherine Hainsworth joined the three men and three women around the long, rectangular table constructed of sturdy light oak polished to a mirror finish.

"Hello, Jack," Catherine said, greeting the purchasing vice president seated to the other side of her. Jack Fatigate, a new hire, was to pull together the purchasing for all the departments into one cohesive project. "Any word yet on why the police are here?"

"Someone found a body behind one of the dumpsters," Jack replied.

"Looks like we're all here," Russell said. "Before we get to the meeting's agenda, let me fill you in on the situation outside. It seems a member of the night cleaning crew was found behind the dumpster next to the building. At the change in the security shift, the new guard took a walk around the building and found the body while we were at the groundbreaking. He notified the police right away. He was shot, and his pockets were emptied of whatever he was carrying. The police took the body to the Volusia County Morgue to verify his identification and to perform an autopsy."

Russell, his salt and pepper hair slightly mussed, paused to take a sip of coffee—he needed to collect himself. A tough businessman on the outside, the murder of his wife several months ago had taken a toll on him. This violence once again reminded him of that awful day. He also felt personally responsible for the safety of his employees.

"I'll keep you informed as we learn more about this unfortunate incident. Right now, it looks like a random robbery gone bad—someone in the wrong place at the wrong time. However, we can't be sure. The body was dragged behind the dumpster probably in an attempt to conceal it, at least for a little while. Ben Sitwell, if you haven't met him yet, is in charge of the building's maintenance and security. He will be installing additional lighting in the parking lot immediately. This murder is very troubling, to say the least."

Russell stared down at the papers in front of him. Visions of his wife lying on the morgues metal slab swam in front of his eyes. He looked up at the group sitting around the table. "The police will be questioning you, as well as other employees. If you saw anything, or hear of something that might help them find who killed this man, please let me know."

Russell again bent his head down. Straightening up, he said, "Under the circumstances, let's take a break. Please help yourselves to the lunch service outside the conference room. We'll reconvene the meeting in an hour."

Chapter 3

—•••—

WHEN THE TEAM reassembled in the conference room with fresh coffee in hand, Russell stood and snapped on the rear view projector.

The screen displayed an artist's rendering of the entire length of the proposed development with the beach and ocean in the foreground.

"The development includes, but is not limited to, a hotel with a multi-story conference center, two condominium towers, a small shopping mall, and a band shell for concerts. There will also be an upscale restaurant in the hotel, as well as a few cafes in the mall."

"It's quite impressive, Russell, when you see a picture of the whole project," Fatigate said, setting his cup down on the table. Others sitting around the table nodded in agreement.

"The majority of the building designs are complete as they were part of the bid process. The investors are in place—a hotel conglomerate won the bid for the conference center, a New Orleans restaurant group has been contracted for the fine dining, and several boutiques have signed leases for the shopping mall. All will be built strictly to code, and in many instances above, to protect the property from hurricane damage."

"What happened to the structures that were on the beach?" Balfor asked.

"Before the project opened for bids, the city, with the State's help, bought and cleared the land," Russell replied. "There were a few hold outs—a tattoo shop, other small businesses, and some homeowners living on family property. They were offered and finally accepted prices based on the market value at the time. The city has installed construction barriers for safety and security."

"Those barriers sure didn't stop the protestors this morning," Fatigate said, his brow furrowed.

"No they didn't." Russell agreed. "This is the first time, the first of many I might add, that the team has been assembled together."

Everyone turned randomly acknowledging each other—all with pleasant smiles.

"I encourage you to meet individually with each other over the next few days to get better acquainted—you will be spending a lot of time together from here on out. In order to bring this project in on time and on, or under budget, it will require we work as a cohesive team. There will be no heroes, and turf wars will not be tolerated."

Russell advanced the presentation displaying an organization chart. "I must admit that you present an impressive lineup of professionals, a depth of knowledge in your field as well as experience in other departments. Reading from left to right, we have Tom Balfor, project vice president."

Balfor stood. "The new project software has been installed and your departments have been set up," he said. "As of tomorrow, your groups can begin training per the schedule I sent to you by email this morning."

"Thank you, Tom," Russell said. "I believe you've all met the lady to my right. Catherine Hainsworth is S&A's architectural design VP. Her initial work was instrumental in our winning the bid. Due to her creative efforts, she is now in charge of all the architectural schematics and the interior designs, where and if needed."

Catherine, thirty-six, a statuesque blonde, presented an air of competence. A woman in a man's world, she rose to her position, not by climbing a corporate ladder, but was catapulted to the top by her talent and hard work. She was impeccably dressed in a light gray suit. The collar of her white silk blouse outlined the neckline of her suit jacket.

"Thank you, Russell," Catherine said, standing up beside her chair. "The schematics and blueprints will be produced using computer aided design software, generally called CAD. The schematics will be updated as the project proceeds and changes are made. The alterations may, of course, necessitate different or varying quantities of materials."

Russell nodded to Catherine as she sat down. "Jack Fatigate, purchasing VP, is next in line," Russell said. "Jack, do you want to say a word?"

"Yes, I do. The development requirements for each building component will be fed into Tom's project software," Jack said, "then overlaid by my purchasing group. The one thing I will stress is that the system must be updated religiously. We will live, or we will die, by the accuracy of our collective projected need for materials, equipment, and labor."

"Thank you, Jack."

"Have the businesses, which will be located in the development, come up with their money?" Balfor asked.

"Initial funds, ten percent from each corporation, have been received. Vera Fredricks, our chief financial officer, verified these deposits at the end of business yesterday. Vera, please take a bow." Vera stood up. Smiling she gave a quick nod to each member of the team before returning to her seat.

"This brings me to the newest member of our team, Brenda Kittles," Stone said. "Tom and Jack have already been working with Brenda. She brings us computer network security expertise and experience in computer forensics. She is now in the process of updating our computer network and verifying that we have enough storage capacity, speed, equipment, and most of all levels of security to keep our project humming, so to speak. Brenda, would you say a few words about your operation?"

Brenda Kittles, thirty-one, was a stunning woman, a woman exuding confidence. Her shiny black hair formed a smooth cap around her face. Her chocolate skin was flawless, giving even more intensity to her dark eyes. She retrieved the remote from Russell and flipped the screen to a flowchart, depicting an overview of the company's computer security system. She walked to the front of the room, commanding the attention of all present. The black of her pantsuit and high heels was softened with a white silk blouse, the top-three buttons modestly open.

"The computer servers, hubs, and peripherals you see on this diagram are already in place in the computer lab, located in the basement of this building," Brenda reported in a strong yet melodic voice. "Redundancy is built-in with three backup systems, plus simultaneous storage on our leased-line host's equipment. This company is also our internet service provider. Battery backup will automatically be triggered in the event of a power failure. System-wide file backup will be performed twice a day—noon and 12:30 a.m. I'll meet with each of you regularly to help ward off problems. Please let me know immediately if you have an issue that needs to be resolved, or if you experience anything out of the ordinary." Brenda, moving with grace, returned to her chair.

"Thanks, Brenda," Russell said. "As you can see, this project will be totally computerized, thus the need for tight security. Hopefully, the investment in technology will save us money, as well as keep us on schedule. That's it for today. Good luck in each of your endeavors. Let's pull together to create a truly spectacular development."

Leaving the conference room, the team members refreshed their coffee and headed back to their offices. Catherine held back to talk with Russell.

"Russell, I wish you luck in this wonderful venture. It's truly a big day for you," Catherine said, beaming. "I also wanted to let you know I have a doctor's appointment, but I should be back before the end of the day in case you need me."

"Oh, I'm sorry. Nothing serious I hope?"

"No. I'm just feeling a little under the weather."

Chapter 4

— • • • —

CATHERINE HAD THIRTY MINUTES before her appointment with the doctor. She closed the window of her silver BMW and turned the AC up a notch, as she left Stone & Associates. Catherine didn't mind the overwhelming summer humidity in Florida. Instead, she went along with the inevitable, wearing her blonde hair in a tight twist to keep her neck cool.

She couldn't pinpoint what she was feeling, but she knew she was coming down with something. Entering the doctor's waiting room, she signed in and took a seat, absentmindedly flipping through a magazine as she waited. It wasn't long before she was called into the examination room. She changed into the blue flowered johnny gown and ran her fingers over her blonde hair to smooth down any strays.

"Catherine, how nice to see you," Dr. Colton said, as he entered the room. He gave her a brief hug and indicated for her to sit up on the examining table. "

What seems to be the matter with one of my favorite patients? You look beautiful as ever. I must get a copy of your exercise routine. You never seem to gain a pound. At thirty-six I was starting to add an inch here and there." Scanning the records in her patient folder, he said, "You're a little early for your yearly exam I see."

"I know. I've been very tired the last week, and I've had an upset stomach the past few days. I think I'm coming down with a bad cold or the flu. I'm working on a big project with Russell Stone, and I need to be on top of my game."

After examining Catherine, Dr. Colton told her she could get dressed and he'd be back in a few minutes. She put the patient's gown in the receptacle and dressed quickly. *I don't even know why I'm here,* she thought. *I feel super right now.* She sat down on the chair by the doctor's desk just as he re-entered the room.

"So, Doctor, is it Vitamin C or Pepto-Bismol?"

"Neither one, Catherine, but I am going to prescribe rest. Don't push yourself beyond your limits, and I want you to take a good multivitamin."

"Sounds like a good prescription for anyone."

"Ah, yes, but when you're creating a little person it's especially important. Catherine, you're going to have a baby."

"What? But that's—"

"You were about to say?" Dr. Colton asked.

"I was about to say that that's impossible, but I guess it could be true. Dr. Colton, do you really think I'm pregnant? Are you sure?"

"Yes, I'm sure. I'd say you are about three months along. So, Catherine what do you think? Are you happy about this baby?"

Catherine's hand began to shake as she pulled a hanky from her purse. She dabbed her eyes which were beginning to show signs of tearing. "It's a miracle. The father was an agent for Homeland Security. We were trying to figure out how we could be together."

"What do you mean *were*?"

"Hutch was killed recently, protecting thousands of people from a dirty-bomb attack in Belmont, NY. I loved him so much, doctor. The thought of having him with me forever through this little person is beyond wonderful. When can we find out if it's a boy or a girl?" she asked, her heart beating rapidly.

"Whoa. Not so fast. We have to set up a schedule of appointments, and there will be tests along the way. I think we might be able to tell the sex in your fifth or sixth month. The main thing I want you to do is to get your rest and follow my guidelines. There's no reason why you can't continue with your work, but if you get tired take a nap."

"Oh, Dr. Colton, thank you so much," Catherine said, her face flushed.

"You're welcome, and I'll see you next month. In the meantime, be a good girl."

"I will. I will. I'll be the best patient you ever had." Giving her eyes one more dab with the hanky, she left the doctor's office, her face beaming.

Chapter 5

— • • • —

"GOOD AFTERNOON. This is Channel 13 news at four," the pretty Hispanic news reporter said, smiling into the camera.

This morning's groundbreaking ceremony for the Daytona Beach Tower Project was accompanied by protestors and an explosion.

First, the explosion. As you can see in the picture to the right of your screen, Stone & Associates' project team dug in their shovels when suddenly an equipment shed, a few yards down the beach, decided to celebrate. The local fire department was on the scene in minutes and doused the can's celebration.

However, the event had already drawn a group of about sixty protestors before the big bang. Our reporter on the scene, Tanya Garcia, caught the action and interviewed their leader. Here's a clip of that interview."

"Hi," Tanya said, holding a cordless microphone in her hand, "you can see the demonstrators gathered behind me, standing by their green bus. Victoria Standish, the woman with the bullhorn, organized the event. Excuse me, Ms. Standish. I'm from Channel 13 News. Can you tell me why you're protesting here today?"

"Yes, I'd be happy to. The planned construction of a major multiplex development is an affront to every Florida taxpayer," Ms. Standish said. "We all have the right to enjoy this beach and that right will be violated forever, if this construction is allowed to proceed."

"And why is that?" Tanya asked.

"Well, we're already cut off from the access to our beach by the construction barriers you see along the road. We can't drive onto the beach now because of their large equipment, or afterward because of restrictions the developer will probably impose against people who are not visiting the multiplex. In other words, our local citizens will not be able to enjoy the beauty of their own city beach."

"Thank you, Ms. Standish."

"And thank you, Tanya Garcia, from Daytona Beach earlier today. From time to time we'll give you updates as this truly ambitious project proceeds. And now the traffic report."

Chapter 6

—•••—

IT WAS LATE AFTERNOON when Catherine left the doctor's office, so she decided not to return to work. She was happy, flushed with excitement, and bursting to share her news with someone. Her mind was going a mile a minute with plans for the baby. A baby! "Oh, Hutch, my agent, I know you're with me," she said, laying her hand on her stomach. "Just look what we made together."

Turning into her driveway, she knew exactly who she wanted to call to relay her exciting news—Manny, her long time friend, and the person who had comforted her after Hutch was killed. She instantly decided to ask Captain Manny Salinas to be her baby's godfather. Still sitting in the car, she pulled her cell phone out of her purse, found his number, and hit the send button.

"Manny, it's Catherine."

"Cat, what a nice surprise," Manny said, calling her by the pet name he gave her when they first met in high school.

"Manny, I have something to tell you. When can I see you?"

"Well, Peaches and I were about to head home. How about we meet you at my houseboat in, say, thirty minutes? I'll even crack a bottle of wine."

"I certainly look forward to a kiss from that dog of yours, but I'll skip the wine this time. See you in a few."

Catherine walked into the house to freshen up. Lucy, her housekeeper, had left an hour earlier so she had the house to herself. She stepped into the library—she had a strong desire to see her baby's father. There was only one picture of the two of them taken by a wandering photographer at the Inlet Harbor Restaurant on their first date. She had copies made for her bedroom and design studio. Picking up the picture, she ran her finger lovingly over Hutch's face. "My darling, you are going to be a daddy. If you were here, I know you would share my excitement." Still looking at her lover's image, her eyes welled with tears, as her hand sought out the St. Christopher medal hanging from around her neck—the gold medal Hutch had given her after they made love for the first time. It was also the last time he had made love to her, and now she was carrying a little miracle.

Wiping the tears away, she went to her bedroom and quickly changed into white shorts and a coral sleeveless T-shirt. She had one more thing to do before going to see Manny.

She went to the vanity in the dressing room and opened her jewelry box. Picking up a small, purple velvet pouch from the bottom of the case and loosening the drawstring, she carefully dropped the contents into her palm. Gently she picked up the rings—two gold bands, one plain and the other held four one-quarter carat diamonds on each side of a three-carat diamond. The rings, engagement and wedding band, were given to her by her late husband, Peter Hainsworth. It was a year after he died from a sudden heart attack that she had taken the rings off and put them in the velvet pouch, storing them in the back of her jewelry box.

Now with a baby on the way, she thought it would be appropriate to wear the rings again. She felt Peter would approve. They had tried to have a baby, but the years slid by without any children. Smiling, she slipped the rings on her finger, holding her hand up to the light. The diamonds sparkled as the stones' facets caught the late afternoon sunlight streaming in the window.

—•••—

Getting out of her car Catherine was greeted by Manny's black Lab, Peaches, racing toward her up the driveway. Peaches skidded to a stop in front of Catherine, sitting patiently for a pat on the head. Catherine obliged and cooed what a beautiful dog she was. Manny waved to her from the aft deck of his houseboat and helped her aboard when she stepped up from the dock. Peaches did a flying leap to the boat's deck.

"My goodness, you look radiant, Cat. I know you said no wine, so I fixed you a glass of iced tea."

"Thank you. Manny, come sit down by me. I have such incredible news."

"Okay, just let me get the tea. I'll be right back."

Catherine sat down on one of the deck chairs. With the sun sliding down in the west, the temperature had dropped enough to be bearable outside. Still, she fanned herself with a napkin Manny had placed on the small table beside her. She looked out over the river, its current running lazily between her banks. Stretching out her legs and kicking off her sandals, she felt as content as a kitten purring on a pillow.

"Do you still like tea with lemon?" Manny called out from the galley.

"Yes, I do. Thanks for remembering."

Manny emerged from the galley with the tea and a scotch on the rocks for himself. Handing the tea to Catherine, he sat down next to her and took a long sip of his drink. "Now, tell me your news."

"Well, I haven't been feeling well for a couple of weeks so I went to see my doctor today," she said, taking a sip of her lemony-flavored tea.

"Cat, you look terrific. Do you think you're coming down with something?"

No longer able to contain herself, she blurted out, "Manny, I'm going to have a baby. I'm going to have Hutch's baby."

"Wait a minute. Cat, are you sure? I mean...you and Hutch—"

"I know what you're thinking. We only knew each other a few months but, but, Manny, we loved each other almost from the moment we first met at the Chamber of Commerce Charity Ball. Remember? You were there." Catherine leaned forward looking into his eyes, willing him to recall the evening.

"Of course, I remember. How could I forget that tango we shared?" Draining his glass, he thought, *I also fell in love that night, with you, Catherine Hainsworth, but I guess I loved and lost you in the span of one evening.* Manny felt his heart stop beating, his unrequited love now seemed even further from his reach.

"Hutch was trying to figure out how we could be together," Catherine continued in a soft voice. "This little miracle was made four days before he died." A lump formed in her throat thinking of her lover. Again, a tear meandered down her check.

"Well, Cat, you're carrying a special gift, a special gift indeed," Manny said, pulling a handkerchief from his pocket and gently wiping the tear away from her face.

"I'm sorry, Manny, I didn't mean to cry. I'm happy. I really am. It's just that the news of this baby is a little overwhelming. You and I are so close. I had to tell you."

"I'm glad you did," he said, putting the handkerchief in her hand. "Now, young lady, let's talk shop here. I don't know anything about a pregnant woman. My wife and I were never so blessed. I want you to know that if there's anything, anything you need, anytime, you must promise you'll call me. I want to be part of this little person's life. Do you hear me?"

"Yes, I hear you. And thank you," she said, picking up his hand, giving it a tender squeeze.

Manny set his glass down, leaned over and kissed Catherine on the cheek. "Promise me you'll let me know if I can help in any way?" Manny said, looking into her radiant brown eyes, a glow emanating from her whole being. Noting the brilliant flash from the diamonds on her finger in the late afternoon sun, Manny suddenly felt a pang of self-doubt. How could he have ever thought of asking this woman to marry him?

"I promise. Actually, I do have a request. It certainly is a different subject, but in a way it's not. Having found myself in the middle of two shootouts, when you and Hutch were bringing down those awful men, unexpectedly involved I might add, I've been feeling rather vulnerable. Now that I'm pregnant, I feel even more so. I live in that big house by myself. Of course, that's going to change, but I'd like you to recommend a small handgun I could keep in my nightstand."

"Have you ever used a gun, Cat?"

"Peter owned a couple of revolvers. He kept them locked in a safe in the library. A few months before he had his heart attack, he took me to a practice range to show me how to fire one of them. I don't remember much. Could you give me a refresher lesson, captain?"

"I'm sure that can be arranged," he said, giving her hand a pat. "Would you like me to stop by on Saturday morning? If I think another weapon would be easier to handle, we can go to the gun shop. They should have just what you need."

"Saturday sounds perfect," Catherine replied. "So, you think it's a good idea?"

"Actually, I do. I do understand. How about eleven o'clock? I'll meet you at your house. Then if you want to see more of a selection, we can go to the gun shop. If you're a good girl, I'll even take you to lunch."

"Oh, I'll be good, captain. Give me a call if you have to chase some robbers. Otherwise I'll see you at eleven," she replied with a broad smile.

— • • • —

Manny walked Catherine to her car, waved goodbye, and returned to his boat. Pouring a double scotch on the rocks, he sat in his favorite spot, the spot where Catherine had shared her news with him. "She seems happy about becoming a mother, Peaches," he said, talking to his dog. "Maybe I do have a chance to be part of her life—a part of her new family. After all, a child should have a father figure don't you think? Something else, Peaches. I'm not going to finish the bottle off tonight. No more of this shit. If I'm going to help her through this, I have to be ready when she calls."

Chapter 7

— • • • —

THE MORNING AFTER Stone & Associates' groundbreaking ceremony, Manny entered the Daytona Beach Police Department and headed to his office area, dubbed the bullpen. He still wore a warm smile after learning of Catherine's pregnancy, and feeling a chance to play a bigger part in her life.

His two detectives, Fred Watson and George Anderson, had their noses into their respective computer screens. The third member of his team, Sergeant Dani Trotter, turned to face Manny as he entered the area with Peaches. Peaches laid down on her pillow next to Manny's desk, and Dani took a long swig on her extra-large Dunkin coffee. Extra large because she instinctively knew this was going to be a long day.

Manny threw his car keys on his desk, picked up a special marker pen and walked to the electronic whiteboard. Not much was left on the board, because the group had just wrapped up a big case. Nevertheless, he hit the save button. LEDs flickered indicating the information on the board was being saved to a file. When the lights ended their dance, Manny wiped the board clean, then leaned against the wall to the right side of the board and faced his team. Swiveling their chairs in his direction, they were certain they were going to learn how he wanted them to proceed with the investigation of the murder on S&A's property.

"A bad couple of events occurred at Stone & Associates yesterday—a murder and an explosion," Manny said, looking into his team's attentive faces. "Random acts? Random robbery gone bad? Accidental explosion of a gas can? The work of some disgruntled activists who want to preserve the beach area? Maybe! George, after the fireman called, asking us to check out the construction-site fire, you went over to have a look. What did you find?"

Manny recruited George, twenty-nine, six-foot-one, white officer, from the Detroit Police Department. George had worked the streets as a detective.

"I met with the fire chief on the beach before he left the scene. We'll have his report shortly," George said. "We did find a very small stain of what could have been an accelerant—it smelled like lighter fluid. I say could have been. The spot was so small, the fire so hot, that not much was left."

"Was there enough for Dani to test," Manny asked.

"Barely. I scooped up the ashes with the stain and brought it back for Dani to analyze. Other than that, we found nothing suspicious, nothing that might have triggered the explosion. The gas can was so badly damaged we couldn't tell if the cap was on or off before it exploded, nor did we find a cap."

"Dani, what kind of a petroleum product was it?" Manny asked.

Sergeant Dani Trotter, twenty-four, had been recruited by Manny fresh out of college. Her job was researcher and lab tech, and whatever else the team needed to have done. She knew she had to pay her dues as the youngest member of the team.

"It definitely was a petroleum distillate product," Dani said. "The kind you buy to fill a cigarette lighter. George said he gave me the entire amount he found. It was hardly enough to have ignited a gas can from the heat of the day, but the spot may have been left behind when the can exploded. Of course, we don't know how much gas was in the can before it blew."

"Fred, what have you come up with regarding the murdered cleaner?" Manny asked.

Detective Fred Watson, black, late thirties, six feet tall, carried a large muscular frame. He wasn't fat by any means. His workout routine kept him rock hard. He was a perfect foil for George. They often used the carrot-and-stick method of interrogation. Fred wielded the stick.

"I've been working with Ben Sitwell, Stone's head of building security," Fred said. "There was no ID on the body. His pockets were picked clean—his wallet was missing, as well as his watch. Naturally, Ben knew who the guy was. He worked for the cleaning company for a couple of years without incident. What I'm getting at, is that he was a trusted employee. So trusted he had a set of keys for the building as well as a master key to the interior office doors that had locks on them. There are four offices with keypads—Stone, Hainsworth, Fredricks, and Kittles. You have to know the code to open their doors."

"How long had this cleaner been carrying the keys?" George asked.

"I asked Ben that very question. He checked his logbook, which showed he had signed out the keys to the cleaner four months ago. The keys were also missing. I checked with the medical examiner, and he said it was a 9mm slug that did him in. Shot in the back. He said he'd have a full report to us soon."

"I did receive a report from Sam," Manny said, "but other than the bullet hole at close range, there wasn't much else he could add—no marks on his body, or signs of a struggle."

"So, we don't have much to go on," Fred continued, after taking a swallow of his tepid coffee. "The cleaner didn't seem to have any enemies. Nothing besides the body, and a lot of blood, were found at the crime scene. Dani dusted the side door for prints, but most were partials because of the grimy surface." Fred, finished with his report, drank the last of his now cold coffee.

"The prints I did get," Dani said, "I ran through the state database and nothing emerged as a match."

"Well, something's going on, but I don't know what," Manny said. "George, you stay with explosion. Get the footage from Channel 13 news that they shot yesterday at the groundbreaking. Take a look to see if anything, or anyone, looks suspicious. Maybe you can spot one of the protestors performing an act of skullduggery before the groundbreaking ceremony, or before the can blew. Dani, call the *News Journal* and ask for copies of the pictures they took as well."

"I'm on it," Dani said. Her face, framed with shoulder-length black hair highlighted with blonde streaks, displayed a keen intent to get to work on her assignment.

"Fred, you head up the murder investigation. Get in touch with Stone's security head again, that Sitwell guy. Ask him if there are cameras anywhere, or a record of people entering or leaving the building. I didn't see a camera where the victim was found when I was over there, but ask him anyway. Find out who generally comes in early or stays late. Talk to them. Did they see anything? That's a wrap for now. Keep your eyes open and your brains cranking."

Chapter 8

— ● ● ● —

CATHERINE WOKE UP the next morning to the usual sunshine streaming through the lace curtains in her bedroom, but her world was different today. She rolled over on her side and drawing the pillow tight against her body. Looking at the picture on her nightstand, a duplicate of the one in the library, she whispered, "My wonderful agent, we're going to have a baby." Most mornings she awoke to a hollow feeling, but this morning she put her hand on her flat belly and warmth spread throughout her body, as she lay looking at Hutch.

Then it was up and at 'em. "Lots to do today, girl," she mumbled, stepping into the shower. Before she knew it she was at S&A asking Maggie if she could see Russell for a minute. Before Maggie could buzz him, Russell entered the doorway to his office.

"Catherine, hello. You look radiant this morning. No more flu?"

"That's what I want to talk to you about," she said, following him into his office. "Russell, I never had the flu," she said softly, a smile spreading across her face. "I'm going to have a baby."

"Hey, slow down. I didn't even know you were seeing someone."

"I'm sure you met him. He was the Homeland Security agent, Stephen Hutchinson, who was instrumental in capturing Douglas Bradshaw."

"Oh, yes, I do remember meeting him," Russell said, "yet, I believe it was before Bradshaw's arrest. He sat at our table at the charity ball. My, that event seems like a long time ago, but it hasn't even been six months."

"I'm sorry, Russell. I know Douglas Bradshaw is a painful subject for you."

"Yes, Catherine, he is. I miss Julie every day. The pain hasn't left me. He's an awful man. He not only killed my precious Julie, but also those three hapless Mexicans he hired illegally on his construction sites."

Catherine could see the torment in Russell's eyes, and etched into the lines of his handsome face, by his wife's premature death.

"Sorry, Catherine," Russell sighed. "I try not to think about that miscreant. You know he stole our plans for the tower project. We won the contract in spite of Bradshaw's efforts at sabotage. Well, enough about him. I do remember the agent you're talking about. But, Catherine, isn't Stephen Hutchinson the man who was killed in New York?"

"Yes...he's the one." Catherine felt a sudden catch in her throat, but willed herself not to cry. "We met during Julie's case. We were drawn to each other instantly. Russell, I swear I fell in love with him the moment I first laid eyes on him," she said wistfully. Catherine could still feel the skip of her heartbeat when she walked up to Hutch and introduced herself at the ball. "Like you, I can't really talk about his death. The hurt is still too raw."

"I know what you mean," Russell said. "I feel the same about Julie, but enough of the past. Tell me more about your news. You're obviously happy and excited about your pregnancy."

"Yes, I am. I'll now have a part of Hutch with me forever. And that is what brought me to your office this morning. My doctor says I can maintain my work schedule. The only caveat is that if I get tired I should rest. In other words, I must listen to my body," she said appearing upbeat again, pushing away the sadness from a moment earlier. "From time to time I may do some of the design touches from my home studio."

"Thank God you're going to continue with the project. You had me worried there for a minute. I've come to depend on you, Catherine, not only for your leadership of the design team, but also your advice and counsel. I guess this is as good a time as any to let you know of my plans. In light of your coming family, I want to know if our long-range goals can dovetail. Do you have time now?"

"Of course, I do, Russell."

"Please have a seat, Catherine. Would you like a cup of coffee? It may take me a little time to tell you what I have in mind."

"Yes, please, but make mine tea. Maggie knows how I like it."

Catherine observed Russell as he poked his head out the door and asked Maggie to bring in the tea and coffee. She also noticed he seemed serious, but not in a sad way, as when he talked about his late wife. In fact, his mood seemed to have lightened considerably. Russell gently closed his office door and came over to sit on the plush green couch facing Catherine across the glass coffee table, floating on its chrome base.

"I've admired your work since I first saw some of your designs for your husband's real-estate clients," Russell said. "While it was a very hard time for you when he died so suddenly, the good news for me was that you sought work at Stone & Associates to help fill the empty spot in your life."

"Your job offer came at just the right time, Russell. I will always be grateful to you for taking a leap of faith with me."

A soft knock on the door announced that Maggie was entering with their tea and coffee. She set the tray down on the coffee table.

"Catherine," Maggie said with a faint Irish brogue, "if there's anythin' else I can get you, let me know."

"Thank you, Maggie," Catherine said, picking up her teacup and adding a wedge of lemon.

Maggie left the two with their private conversation, closing the door behind her.

"Maggie still has a hint of her Irish brogue," Catherine said, stirring her tea. "I enjoy listening to her speak."

Russell paused, taking a long sip of his coffee. Setting it down on the glass, he leaned forward with an earnest look on his face. "I have something to say to you, Catherine, and I'm glad for this opportunity to tell you about my plans."

"I'd love to hear about them."

"Catherine, the tower project will probably take the firm the better part of two years, and depending on unforeseen circumstances, maybe even three. When the multiplex development is completed, I plan to retire. Who knows, maybe I'll even find myself an island somewhere, but, yet, not too far from Florida," he said, with a slight shake of his head.

A smile crossed his face, and Catherine saw a hint of sparkle in his eyes. "Russell, that sounds like a heavenly and well-deserved goal," Catherine said, taking a sip of her tea.

"But—" Russell paused again.

"But. Go on, Russell. I can tell by your face, there's more." She was entranced with his revelation of his plans to retire.

"Catherine, I'm offering you a partnership in the firm. Now. Right now. Today even, if you say yes, but I'm sure you'll want to hear me out first. At the completion of the project, Stone & Associates will be regarded as one of the preeminent architectural firms in the world. I want you to be ready to take the helm when I retire."

Not much ever surprised Catherine. Being the daughter of a naval officer who became an astronaut, and a mother who played first chair violin for the Florida Symphony, she was not often caught off guard by what might come next. But Russell's offer of a partnership, let alone to take over the reins of the firm, had never entered her mind.

"Russell, I don't know what to say." She set her cup down and looked wide-eyed at him. "I'm honored, but to fill your shoes—"

"Nonsense. You're perfect. Your training and knowledge of building and architectural design is far above anyone I've ever met, and then there are your people skills. I've seen how you work with your staff, how you've worked with the town's movers and shakers in pulling off their agreement to develop projects in the city, heck, even in the *State*. I know with the pending birth of a new Hainsworth, it must seem like a lot at one time, but it will be two to three years before you'll take over. The little one would no longer be an infant. What do you say? Will you consider my offer of a full partnership in the second love of my life, Stone & Associates?"

"Of course, I'll consider your offer, Russell. I'd be a fool not to. I have to admit, that since working for you, I've dreamed of establishing my own design firm. But, that was it, a dream."

"Maybe I can make your dream come true."

The enormity of the words Russell had spoken to her, were whirling in Catherine's head. Two incredible pieces of news within two days time were unbelievable. Catherine drank the last of her tea, set her cup down on the tray, and stood up. Russell did the same.

"Russell, I thank you for the offer, and it's an honor that you would extend a partnership to me in this truly amazing company. Please give me some time, because, of course, I now have someone else I must consider in my life's decisions," Catherine said, extending her hand.

He took her hand in both of his. "It is I who will be honored, Catherine, if you accept my offer."

Catherine started to walk to the door but stopped abruptly. She turned around quickly. "Russell, I almost forgot a question I was going to ask you when I first came in. As I said, I may work from home occasionally, but I don't think my computer can handle the CAD program. I'll need a different machine, or at least upgrade the one I have with more storage and speed. I'm not quite sure what I need. Can I ask Brenda Kittles for suggestions and help?"

"Of course. In fact, whatever she thinks you need, I'll ask her to order the equipment and to install it. She'll make sure it's compatible with our system and set up the network connection. I'll call her right now. Catherine, if there is anything else I can do to make work easier for you, please let me know."

"Thanks, Russell." The two friends hugged briefly.

— •••—

Everything is going to work out, she thought, as she turned down the hallway heading to Brenda Kittles' office.

Brenda was delighted to hear Catherine's news of the coming baby. She suggested they get started right away on the upgrade to her home computer. "Catherine, I was going to start another task, but how about we check out what you need first. I could meet you at your house in an hour, if that's convenient?"

"Perfect. Don't eat anything before you come over. I'll ask Lucy, my housekeeper, to fix us a little lunch."

Most of the staff, as well as Brenda, knew Catherine was special to Stone & Associates. So if she needed something, she usually got it right away. What nobody knew was that Stone had just offered Catherine a partnership in the company.

Chapter 9

— • • • —

CATHERINE RUSHED HOME to straighten up her studio before Brenda arrived. Pushing the button on her intercom to the kitchen, she called out, "Lucy, are you there?"

"Yes, Miss Catherine. You're home early. Would you like a bite of lunch?"

"That would be wonderful, but please make a couple of extra sandwiches. I have a guest coming over in thirty minutes, Brenda Kittles from Stone & Associates. Oh, and, Lucy, would you put a glass of milk on the tray for me? I'm not sure what Brenda would like to drink with her sandwich. Wait to bring up the tray, and we'll ask her when she gets here."

Thirty minutes later the front door chime signaled that Brenda had arrived just when she said she would.

"Hello," Lucy said, opening the door wide for her to enter. "I'm Lucy, Miss Catherine's housekeeper, and you must be the lady she's expecting."

"Hi, and, yes, I have an appointment with Catherine. My name is Brenda Kittles." She extended her hand to Lucy already liking what she saw.

Lucy was dressed in a uniform of sorts, wearing a light gray dress covered with a white bib apron. Her practical black shoes anchored her medium-sized frame to the white tiled floor. But it was her eyes that captivated Brenda. They were blue and seemed full of laughter. Her reddish-brown hair curled around her face, framing apple cheeks and sweet pink lips smiling at Brenda.

"It's nice to meet you, Miss Kittles."

"Please, call me Brenda."

"Ah, Brenda, come along. We have a bit of a climb because Miss Catherine's design studio is on the third floor."

They topped the landing to the studio, and Catherine came over to greet her guest. "Hi, Brenda. Come on in and look around. Lucy's making some sandwiches for lunch, if that's okay with you?"

"Sounds wonderful. I have to get back to work when we finish here to install more memory on Jack Fatigate's system," Brenda said. "I wasn't going to get a chance to eat, but you mentioned we might grab a bite together."

"What would you like to drink?" Catherine asked. "I'm having milk, but we have coffee, or tea with ice if you like."

"Iced coffee would be terrific. Thanks, Lucy. Coming from Alaska, I'm still not used to this Florida heat, to say nothing of the humidity."

"Iced coffee it is," Lucy said, pursing her lips into a bow. "I'll be back shortly with your lunches."

"Catherine, this is quite a layout you have here. I love the space—so many windows. I see your computer system. Do you mind if I check it out?"

"Not at all. It's on, so have at it."

"Do you have access to our server at S&A?"

"No, I never really needed to. I keep a backup of my design files on a portable hard drive and transfer any new documents and updates to my system when I'm at the office."

"I see you have a modem," Brenda said, pulling the chair away from the desk so she could see underneath. "For security purposes, and to make it easier to backup your work, I think I'll fix you up with a different modem and set the connection so you can download your CAD files directly to our company's server."

"I won't even pretend to say I understand everything about the system. But I do understand the overall picture. Some of the terminology is new to me."

"No problem. I'll upgrade your equipment. You need more RAM and a bigger hard drive—more storage capacity. Those CAD files you create are storage hogs. I see you have a twenty-one inch monitor. Is that a large enough screen for you?"

"Well, now that you ask, I was thinking of getting a bigger one, so I don't have to scroll around so much."

"Russell said to order whatever you need, so let's go for it," Brenda chuckled, looking up at Catherine with a smile.

The kitchen intercom beeped and Catherine pressed the button on her unit. "Hi, Lucy. Is our lunch ready?"

"It sure is. Do you and Miss Brenda want to eat upstairs or down here in the library?"

"Great idea, Lucy. The library. We'll be right down. Thanks."

"Brenda, if you have all the information you need we'll go downstairs, a little easier going down than up three flights."

"Yes, I have everything," Brenda said, following Catherine down the stairs to the library on the first floor.

Lucy put the lunch tray on the gleaming cherry butler's table between the caramel-colored leather couch and two matching recliners.

The two new friends fixed their plates from the tray, selecting from Lucy's open-faced salmon sandwiches on cucumber and cream cheese, topped with tiny sprigs of dill. Brenda added a spot of cream to her iced coffee, and the two women sat back to enjoy their lunch.

"Do you eat like this all the time?" Brenda asked taking a bite of the little sandwich.

"Lucy is a jewel, and she particularly likes preparing food, with her own flair, when I have guests," Catherine said. "Tell me, Brenda, if you don't mind my asking, how did you happen to land in Daytona Beach?"

"Well, as you can imagine, studying computer science, with a concentration in computer forensics, took a number of years. Then I had to add some experience before any company would even look at me. But one offered me an entry-level job, so I could get some experience."

"Sounds like they make you jump through hoops," Catherine said, taking a sip of milk.

"To get the experience, they started me setting up a couple of small firm's computer security systems. I was also a backup on a case where a hacker got into a system and destroyed some files. That is, the hacker thought he destroyed the files, but there are usually ways to retrieve the information."

"I've heard that, but I hope I never have to prove it."

"Then a couple of months ago I saw an ad for a computer security and network specialist at S&A. The rest, shall we say, is history."

"I know Russell thinks highly of you. By the way, anything you need, even if it's just a dinner companion, please ask me," Catherine said, finishing her glass of milk.

"Thank you, Catherine. I don't know anybody in the area, and my family lives in Alaska, which seems like a world away," Brenda said, her face frowning momentarily.

"I take it you're not married. Any significant other?"

"Lord, no. No time for that stuff. I barely have time to brush my teeth, what with all the journals to read, and bulletins that keep hitting my inbox with the latest in computer technology."

"Where are you staying, Brenda? You and I have talked over the past few weeks, but we haven't had a chance for some good, old-fashioned girl talk."

"Funny you should ask," Brenda said. "I've been so busy setting up S&A's security system that finding a nice place to live just hasn't risen to the top of my priority list. Right now I'm in a summer rental on the beach. Trouble is I feel like I'm living out of a suitcase. I'll have to do something soon, because the rent will skyrocket when the snowbirds start returning for their winter retreat. But I have so much work to do—"

"Oh, wait a minute, Brenda, I have an idea. Come stay with me until you have the time to look around. I have this huge house with plenty of room. I'd love to have you. Lucy would see to it that we both have hot meals or cold, with this summer heat touching a hundred. You would have the run of the house. Your being here would be like having a sister. Who knows, maybe I'm building a family from the top down and the bottom up," Catherine laughed.

"Catherine, that's an incredibly generous offer, but I'm afraid I would really be imposing."

"Not at all! There are four big bedrooms in this house plus mine. It's about time I put them to use. One bedroom is across the hall from my room. I was thinking of converting it to a nursery so the baby will be close to me. Listen to me. I can't believe I'm having a baby," Catherine said, and hurried on. "There is a bedroom next to *the nursery* with a bathroom in-between. I'm going to ask Lucy to move in with me. Please don't say a word about the baby because I haven't told her anything yet. I just hope she'll say yes. She'd make a wonderful nanny." Catherine put down her empty plate, looking intently at Brenda.

"Brenda, before you say another word, come with me. I want to show you the bedrooms on this floor with a private bath."

"Your house is really lovely, and it certainly seems like it'll expand to accommodate your upcoming needs," Brenda said with a wink.

"Oh, I think it will, too. Now, what do you think of this layout?"

"Catherine, what a wonderful space. The room is huge, and look at this dressing room—it makes an alcove with the bay window. Catherine, I can't refuse your offer. Do you know how wonderful this nook would be for my laptop, and all this room, and look at this bathroom. It's beautiful," Brenda exclaimed, darting from one area to the next.

"Well, it doesn't have a tub," Catherine called to her, "only a shower, but there's lots of cupboard space. The vanity is smaller than upstairs, but on the other hand it would be private."

Brenda continued to stroll around the room.

"If Lucy accepts my offer, we three girls would be great companions, but with the layout of the house each of us will have our own space. So, are you saying yes, Brenda? I hope."

"Yes. Yes. And yes. Can I move in this weekend? My rental is tenant at will, week-to-week, or am I rushing you?"

"Are you kidding? This weekend would be perfect. Tell you what, why don't you come over for dinner tonight. I'll have told Lucy about the baby by then, and asked her if she'll move in with us. If she says yes, we'll have a celebration, get better acquainted, and make plans. If she says no...well, I won't accept no," Catherine said, eyes wide. "So we'll definitely celebrate and settle the details for your move Friday or Saturday or whenever you wish."

"Whoa, one thing, miss benefactor, I insist on paying you rent."

"No, no, this is my pleasure."

"No, no, yourself. I pay you rent or I don't move in. There'll be an extra food expense, utility costs, to say nothing of the pain and suffering of putting up with me. You don't know, I may have some weird habits you can't stand. I'll pay you rent, and we'll say it's month-to-month so you can throw me out if I'm too much. After all, you're planning to add two adults and baby to a space that you've enjoyed on your own."

"Truth be told, Brenda, I was very lonely after Peter died, but then my work helped ease the feeling of isolation. Of course, Lucy's been a big help. When Hutch came into my life, everything seemed to change. I was so happy. But then he was so abruptly taken from me that this empty house was beginning to feel like a millstone around my neck."

"I know what you mean, the lonely part. Catherine, I'd love to join you for dinner, and to celebrate a new beginning—so many new beginnings. I can probably be back about 5:30. Is that okay?"

"Perfect. Thanks, Brenda for saying yes." Catherine gave her new roommate a hug. "See you later."

—•••—

"Lucy, are you in the kitchen? Stay there if you are. I have some big news for you and a proposal."

"Yes, Miss Catherine. I'm just finishing the lunch dishes."

Catherine breezed into the kitchen. "Lucy, please come with me to the library. There seems to be positive energy in there today."

"All right, but I'm not quite finished here."

"Not to worry, Lucy, come along." They entered the library which was now cool as the sun's rays where low on the west side of the house.

"Lucy, I have three things to tell you. Well two things to tell you, and one thing to ask you. First, and the biggest news of all, I'm going to have a baby."

"What? How? I mean...Miss Catherine, the only man you've really been seeing was Agent Hutch, and Oh, Miss Catherine—"

"Don't say it, Lucy," Catherine said, raising both hands in the air, "and, yes, Hutch is the father of my baby. Lucy, I'm so very happy."

"Oh, Miss Catherine, then I'm excited for you. When?"

"Dr. Colton, I saw him yesterday, thinks around late January. Now, that brings me to what I want to ask you, Lucy. I've been mulling over an idea in my mind for quite a while, several months actually. Now, I know it's the right time and the right thing to do. Lucy, you live alone, and your family is gone, much like me. So it's silly for us to live apart when I have this great big house. Lucy, will you move in with me? Will you help me with the baby?"

"Oh, Miss Catherine, do you mean it, and a baby—"

"If it turns out to be too much for you, we can either hire a nanny or we can hire a housekeeper, whichever way you want. The bedroom across from mine will make a perfect nursery. Don't you agree?"

"Oh my, yes. A wonderful nursery."

"And, as you know, the adjoining bathroom leads into another large bedroom. That would be your room, but the whole house will be your home. What do you think?"

"Miss Catherine, this is so much to take in. You know I love you like a daughter—now a baby on the way. I always wanted to take care of an infant. Are you sure you want me to help with such a treasure?"

"I can't think of another soul I would trust more with my baby than you. Please say yes."

"Oh, oh, Miss Catherine," Lucy said, pulling a hanky out of her apron pocket, dabbing tears from her eyes, "it would be an honor to help you. And, the thought of living in this beautiful house with such a kind lady, and a new baby, is truly overwhelming. Yes, my answer is a *big* yes."

Catherine went to Lucy's side, put her arms around her in a warm hug.

Lucy gave her nose a gentle blow into her hanky, and then tucked it back into her apron pocket. "You said you had two things to tell me."

"Yes, I do have one more piece of information. It has to do with the woman you just met, Brenda Kittles."

"She seems very nice and so pretty. She certainly loved the lunch I fixed. Ate both sandwiches."

"Brenda is head of computer security at Stone & Associates. She moved here from Washington DC, but she's originally from Alaska. Because of all the preparations for the new construction, she hasn't had a chance to find a place to live. She's been renting an apartment week-to-week on the beach side. I've asked her to stay with me, here, until she decides where she wants to live. Lucy, she said yes. I offered her the bedroom suite on the first floor. She loved it. Lucy, I hope you like the idea. What do you think? Honestly."

"I think a guest in the house is terrific," Lucy answered. "She being a colleague of yours is almost like family. What a wonderful household we're going to have."

Chapter 10

—•••—

BRENDA ENTERED S&A's computer lab. Her domain. Her mood was upbeat, a spring in her step. She still couldn't believe her good fortune that Catherine had invited her to stay in her home until she found something more permanent. Dinner last night with Lucy and Catherine had been delightful. The three bonded like school girls.

Flicking on the lab's fluorescent lights, she heard a ping from the computer. Looking over her shoulder at the monitor, as she put her purse and an armful of papers on the table by the door, she was startled to see an unusual message with large white letters on a crimson background.

> *"Good morning, Brenda. I have an aversion to playing cat and mouse, so I thought you and I might play a game of chess. I'll return soon to explain the rules. Have a nice day."*

The message filled the screen and didn't look to have come in through her email. With no buttons displayed to click, Brenda pressed the CTRL and P keys simultaneously to print the message. The printer did not come to life. The message disappeared along with a faint laugh which emanated from the speakers embedded in the monitor. The lab silent except for the slight hum of the equipment.

"What kind of a prank is this?" she mumbled.

Brenda logged into her corporate email account to check if the strange message was listed. The inbox contained several new messages but nothing unusual.

The buzzer at the lab's door signaled someone wanted to gain access. Brenda could see through the door's window that Detective Fred Watson had pushed the button. Annoyed at being interrupted in her search for the genesis of the peculiar message, she went to the door and punched the intercom button. "Good Morning, detective. Can I help you with something?"

"Yes, I'd like to talk to you. May I come in?" Fred asked, his arm up leaning into the door.

Brenda hit the release button allowing the door to open. Fred entered the lab and gave a soft whistle as he looked around at the equipment. "Very impressive. Did you assemble all this yourself?"

"Yes I did. Now what can I help you with? I have to get back to work," Brenda said, her mind wandering back to the message.

"Seems I caught you at a bad time." Fred noted the frown and the troubled look on her face. "I'd like to ask you a few questions pertaining to the murdered cleaning man. I promise it won't take long. I'm interviewing Mr. Stone's staff, and you're first on my list."

"Sure. Sure. Go ahead."

"I want to check the lab's security. Actually, it's not specific to just the lab. I'm checking all the sensitive areas, Stone's office, as well as everyone on his direct staff."

Brenda didn't seem to be listening to him. She'd returned to the monitor and was rapidly opening and closing screens.

"Miss Kittles, do you want me to come back?"

"Uh, no. What did you say, detective?"

"Please, call me Fred. I asked if you would like me to come back at another time."

Brenda swung around giving the detective her full attention.

"I'm sorry, Fred...you can call me Brenda. A goofy message was displayed on my monitor when I walked in this morning. Nothing sinister really, but I'm not sure how it got there."

"Well, I'll leave you to your search. I know when a computer geek is on the hunt it's best to clear the area."

"Excuse me. Computer geek?" she snapped. *He has some nerve,* she thought.

"Well, I didn't mean that in a derogatory way. Tell you what. I'll leave you, the computer expert, to your investigation, if you'll have dinner with me tonight."

"My, my, detective. Are you asking me for a date or a business meeting?"

"Well, definitely a date, but I can't promise we won't touch on business. I really would like to get to know you and learn more about this impressive setup."

"Are you asking all of Mr. Stone's staff members out to dinner?"

"No, Miss Kittles, just you," Fred said smiling, but with a quizzical look, brows furrowed.

"Fred, I don't date. A business meeting over dinner, on the other hand, is very appealing. Do you still want to meet for dinner?"

"You drive a hard bargain, Miss Kittles, but yes, I'll agree to that. How about six o'clock. We're both in town so it would be silly to go home for an hour. How about I pick you up here at six? Is the building open or should I wait for you out front?"

"You really are presumptuous, detective. We don't lock up the building until seven. Tell me the name of the restaurant where you'd like to have dinner and I'll meet you there."

"Brenda, do you think I'm a monster? I promise I'm not going to attack you. But yes, I'll meet you at the Aquarium at six. I'll make reservations for us, if that's okay with you? They get busy with the business crowd at that hour."

"That's okay with me. Will the reservation be under your name?"

"Yes, unless you would rather have it under Kittles." Fred was starting to get annoyed.

"What is your last name?"

"Watson."

"Oh, very funny. Like in Sherlock Holmes and Dr. Watson!" she said sarcastically.

"No. Like in Fredrick James Watson, Detective, Daytona Beach Police Department. The reservation will be under the name of Watson, my dear."

Fred turned on his heel, left the lab, and the unpleasant woman who worked there.

Brenda picked up the folders she brought to work but continued to ponder about the morning's message, the dinner invitation forgotten. Setting the folders down, she opened her personal logbook. Turning to a fresh page, she wrote: "Thursday morning, 8:32 a.m. Found strange message on my screen when I entered the lab." She completed the entry noting what she remembered of the message and that nothing appeared unusual in her email account.

She then printed the system log file, giving her a list of every event that had taken place in the last twenty-four hours—who logged into the system, what they did, and which programs ran. As she searched the system log file she kept wondering about the message—where did it come from, and who put it there?

Chapter 11

— • • • —

VERA FREDRICKS UNLOCKED the door to her office, entered, and threw her bag on the credenza next to the picture of her husband. Vera, forty-six, was the first employee Stone hired when he formed the company. Her short, curly, prematurely gray hair gave her a friendly, carefree air, but she was a fanatic when it came to balancing the books.

Vera booted up her computer, sipping her coffee as it performed the opening diagnostics. Once the desktop displayed, she smiled at the picture of her twins on her monitor. They were growing up so fast, and now they were leaving the nest. The girls were preparing to enter college. Freshman orientation started in two weeks, so there was much hubbub in the Fredrick's home. "I'm glad you aren't going far, my dears," she said to the picture. Clicking on the spreadsheet icon, the program opened covering the picture of the twins.

After checking some calculations, Vera logged into the corporate bank account at Port Orange City Bank. The bank's welcome screen displayed the standard message: *Last login 3:12 a.m. EST – Russell Stone.*

"What's this? Last login at 3:12 a.m.?" A puzzled look crossed her face. She quickly scanned the overnight deposits. The hotel conglomerate had deposited $1.5 million of their initial working capital to start construction. The hotel's email, indicating this deposit was coming, had been received before the end-of-business yesterday.

Vera called the manager of the bank to see if their log files showed Russell logged in at 3:12 a.m. The manager verified the login had occurred, and that it was Russell Stone. Vera always printed out an end-of-day statement and filed it in her desk drawer. Drinking the remainder of her coffee, she retrieved yesterday's last printout. It matched her spreadsheet entry. She scanned the online account entries again. Everything was in order. With printout in hand, she headed for Russell's office to see if he could clear up the matter.

"Good morning, Maggie. Is Russell in? I'd like to see him a minute."

Russell heard Vera in the outer office and called to her to come on in. "Good morning, Vera. How are you today?"

"I was terrific, but I found a login to our bank account at 3:12 this morning. You didn't happen to walk in your sleep last night did you?" she asked trying to smile.

"No, I don't think so. I've never walked in my sleep before," he said returning what he believed to be Vera's good-natured smile.

"Well, the login record says otherwise, and the bank's record indicates that it was you. Nothing changed in the account. The bank and I balance."

"Well, I did check the account yesterday around mid-afternoon, but certainly not in the middle of the night. Is it possible the computer did a scan and marked my entry at the wrong time?" Russell asked, concern now showing on his face.

"Not likely."

"You've already checked with the bank, so I guess the next step is to see Brenda. Now is the time to clear up any computer glitches with the bank. We're going to have some large amounts deposited soon."

"They've already started, Russell. $1.5 million was deposited last night by the hotel group."

"Good. I saw their email yesterday stating that was their intention. I'd hate to think someone was getting into our bank accounts," he said more to himself than to Vera. "We're going to need every penny for the project, plus the auditor requires an entry for every transaction. Let me know what Brenda finds."

Chapter 12

— • • • —

VERA RODE THE ELEVATOR down to the basement. Outside the computer lab door Vera punched in Brenda's access code. A soft click, and the display of a small green light, signified recognition of the code. Vera opened the door and stepped in. She saw Brenda sitting by a rack of computers humming away—lights flashed randomly, driven by millions of streaming data bits.

Brenda turned when she heard the door open and waved for Vera to come over to the table where she was studying some printouts.

"Hi, Vera. What brings you to my world in the bowels of our company's operation?" Brenda said with a chuckle.

"Well, it may be nothing, but my intuition is niggling me to check."

"Why is that?" Brenda said looking up at Vera's perplexed face.

"This morning when I logged into the company bank account, the welcome message displayed the last login as 3:12 a.m. Brenda, the login indicates it was Russell, or at the very least someone masquerading as him."

"That is odd," Brenda said. And, I had that weird message on my screen.

"Russell asked me to call the bank, which I'd already done. The bank manager checked, and she did find a login at 3:12 a.m. and a logout at 3:14 a.m. attributed to Russell. Our balances still matched so nothing bad happened. Maybe I'm just being paranoid."

"Hang on a minute, Vera. As you say this might be explained away, but I don't like the looks of it, and you're right to be concerned." As she was talking, Brenda sent an email to all employees that the system would shut down for a routine maintenance check in sixty seconds, and to save and close all files immediately. She also included that the system would be back up in twenty minutes. Noting the time clock on her monitor, after sixty seconds she took the machine off-line.

"The first thing I have to do, Vera," Brenda said, as her fingers flew over her keyboard, "is to make a complete system backup to a clean storage disk. The result is a duplicate of the entire system up to the moment I cut the connection."

"I'm glad it's you and not me," Vera said. "The speed you're clicking those keys makes me look like a turtle, and I thought I was fast."

Brenda didn't reply concentrating on the commands she was issuing to the computer. "Once the copy is complete, I'll bring the server backup—the duplication process won't take long. By the way, who've you told about this event?"

"Just Russell and you, and, of course, the bank manager."

"Good. Let's keep it that way for now. You and I may be paranoid, but that's a big part of what we get paid for don't you think?"

"You bet it is. I know people feel that I'm a pain in the butt at times. I guess it goes with the territory," Vera replied.

"Pain in the butt is putting it mildly. I can just see the emails once I bring this baby back online. I'll get back to you later with what I find."

Vera left the lab, but almost on her heels the door swung open again.

"What do you think we've got, Brenda?" Russell asked, joining her.

"I don't know yet. The copy process of the system has just completed, isolating all activity yesterday up to the point when I shut down the network. I'll finish this email notice that the system is back up, and then explain to you what I've done so far." Brenda hit the send button, and then turned to Russell.

"Let me show you my notebook," Brenda said, placing the spiral-bound book in front of Russell. "This is a log of everything I do, a journal of events. Note my second entry starts with the email I sent out stating the system would be down in sixty seconds. It's critical that I document every procedure and step I make."

"Do you keep the printout of the system log file as well?" Russell asked.

"Yes, and I'll reference such in the journal. Now with a duplicate of the system safely stored, I can attempt to reconstruct the chain of events leading to the login message Vera saw on her screen. Russell, did you access the bank account from home yesterday?"

"No. In fact, I never do. I always check the accounts from my office. Are you saying you can tell if I log into the system from home?"

"Yes, because your home computer will leave a different trail, a unique computer ID. I'll review the audit trails of system activity to determine whether the bank account login came from your office computer, or your home computer, or somewhere in the building, or, heaven forbid, out in cyberspace."

"Well, I'll leave you to your analysis. As I told Vera, I wasn't on any computer from the time I left the office yesterday, about 6:00 o'clock, until this morning. Actually this morning, all I did was turn on my PC. Please keep me posted."

Brenda didn't answer. She was already checking the audit trails of the system. Russell left the lab with an uneasy feeling in the pit of his stomach.

Chapter 13

—•••—

RUSSELL HAD NO MORE than left the computer lab when Brenda had another thought. She called his office and asked Maggie to have him call her the minute he stepped back into the office.

"Hang on, Brenda. He just came through the door."

"Yes, Brenda."

"Russell, don't touch anything on your desk. I'd like to have it dusted for prints."

"Okay, I'll call Manny. I'm sure he'll send someone right over, probably that Detective Watson. You may have met him. He's been questioning employees regarding that awful murder."

"I did meet the detective. I hope someone can come over right away. Tell him any delay could compromise a crime scene."

—•••—

Maggie called Brenda to let her know Detective Watson and Sergeant Trotter had arrived, and they were waiting for her in Russell's office. Brenda joined them just as Fred was introducing the young woman with him to Russell and then to her. "You and Dani should get along like two peas in a pod. Dani's computer practically has a nervous breakdown when she's on the hunt for information," Fred said laughing.

"Good to know," Brenda replied smiling, as she shook Dani's hand.

"Brenda, what are we looking for?" Fred asked.

"That's the problem, I don't know. Two unexplained events happened last night on our computers. One incident may have been triggered from Russell's PC. I haven't had time to trace it yet in the system log file. I had this thought that, if an intruder came into Russell's office, the evidence could be compromised before I had time to find the event's origin. I guess we're looking for something that shouldn't be here, if that makes sense, or I've been watching too many cop shows."

"Hey, you can never watch too many cop shows," Dani said, chuckling.

"Oh, oh, somebody else has my addiction," Brenda said. "Here's what I have so far. The bank's system record indicates that Russell logged into the bank account at 3:12 a.m. and off at 3:14 a.m.— Russell was home in bed. I was about to start the analysis of the chain of events when Maggie called that you two had arrived."

"Whoa, Fred, I love this lady. She talks my kind of language. Please continue, dear friend," Dani said grinning from ear to ear.

"We still don't know if there's a logical explanation, but so far none has surfaced—not here or at the bank."

"What's the other event?" Fred asked. "You said there were two."

"Oh, yes...you are listening aren't you?"

"Just doing my job, ma'am," Fred said, enjoying the byplay with Brenda.

"There was a message on my screen when I came into work, nothing alarming, but I'm not sure how it got there. It could be a prank. I already told Fred about it. I had just read the message when he arrived to ask me some questions about the murder."

"What did the message say?" Dani asked.

"Oh, something about playing chess instead of a game of cat and mouse." As Brenda finished giving the group her information, Dani opened her forensic kit with the equipment she needed to dust for prints. She didn't have to take Russell's prints—they were already on file. At the time of his wife's murder he was a *person-of-interest*.

"I'll dust everything on the desk including this keyboard and mouse," Dani said. "Fred, what else do you suggest we check? Doorknobs—"

"You know," Russell interrupted, "I did notice something out of place when I came in this morning. I'm right handed so my mouse is usually to the right side, or close to the center of the monitor. This morning it was to the left of center. I didn't give it a thought at the time, just presumed Maggie moved it straightening my desk. By the way, Fred, is there anything new on the murdered man?"

"Not really. I've been working with Ben Sitwell. I'd like you and Brenda to come with me to talk to him again, if you don't mind, while Dani dusts your office."

— • • • —

Fred and Brenda, led by Russell, headed for the elevator. They rode the car down to the basement and headed to Sitwell's office, located down the hall from Brenda's computer lab.

Ben's office door was open. He looked up as the group entered.

"Excuse us, Ben," Russell said, "I think you already know Detective Watson."

"Yes, we've had a couple of conversations. Nice to see you, detective," Ben said as the two men shook hands.

"We'd like to ask you a couple of questions," Russell said, "regarding the keys you checked out to the cleaner. When did you assign the keys to him?"

"About four months ago," Ben said. "The guy asked if he could have a key to make it easier to dump the trash. He said he was propping the side door open and was concerned some stray animal, cat, armadillo, or a speedy turtle, might get in." Ben grinned at Brenda. He knew she was still becoming acquainted with the local creatures.

Brenda gave a little shudder, but returned his grin.

"I notice that some of the doors in the building have access only when a code is punched in," Fred said. "For instance, Brenda's computer lab has a keypad. And, Mr. Stone, your door is coded. Ben's door is coded, but he mentioned to me it hasn't been operating correctly in the last few weeks. Figures a security guy doesn't think he has anything important," Fred said, smirking at Ben.

"What the hell, your security pad doesn't work?" Russell asked angrily.

"The lock people were busy. They said they would work me in. I'm sorry, Russell. Here are a couple of pieces of information that may or may not fit. I have a notebook on my desk between bookends with lots of other books. The spine of the one I'm thinking about has the word *codes*. It has a list of the codes for the various keypads."

"Ben, does the notebook give names, or departments, or location next to the list of codes?" Russell asked. He was becoming more and more annoyed with his so-called head of security.

"Yes. Both the employee's name, the department, and the office locations are typed next to the code," Ben said, with a crestfallen face. He knew he'd caused a security breach.

"Sometimes it's the obvious we don't see, Ben," Russell retorted.

"Well, there's another thing you're not going to like," Ben said. "I questioned my nightshift guard to see if he saw or heard anything unusual the night of the murder, before his shift ended. He said he hadn't, but then he confessed that he might have nodded off during the wee hours of the morning. He said, after he does his 2:00 a.m. check, he sits in the lobby. Because of the large glass windows he can keep an eye on the street and the front entrance. However, he admitted that at times he dozes off."

"Ben, change the lock on the side door and install a crash bar with a buzzer alert if it's opened. Put up a sign that the door is only to be used in case of an emergency. If someone tries to get in, or out, we'll know," Russell ordered, "and fire that night watchman."

"Yes, sir."

"And, Ben, get your door fixed immediately and change all the keypad access codes. When you give the new codes to those who need to know, tell them it's a routine procedure to periodically change them. Please recode them quarterly from here on, but on a staggered schedule."

"Yes, sir."

—•••—

The group retraced their steps to Stone's office. "Well," Fred said, "given what we heard from Ben, there were all kinds of opportunities for someone to perform a dirty deed." Fred, looking out Russell's office window, turned back to the group. "When you think about what's happened here," Fred said, "there are actually three incidents—the murdered cleaner, the bank login, and Brenda's morning message."

"That's right," Russell said.

"If your nightshift guy dozed off the night of the murder," Fred continued, "we can probably assume that he takes a nap every night. Consequently, if the bad guy has a key to the building and the code to your office, it doesn't take a genius to see how he got into the bank account from your computer, except he would have to know the user ID and password."

"Well, someone," Brenda said, "was into the system last night in order to leave me that message. If he was smart enough, truly computer savvy at a system level, he could open the system's password file which would give him access to everyone's space on the server as well as the bank account."

Dani looked up. "In my experience, there aren't many who are that sophisticated a user. But, if they are that knowledgeable, they would be canny enough to erase their tracks when they leave."

"Mr. Stone, let's operate on the assumption that the murder and a potential hacker into your operation are connected," Fred said. "In which case, I'd like to proceed with the investigation on a need-to-know basis. You may have an employee who is scheming to do you harm, or, at the very least, your company."

"I agree," Russell answered. "Dani, let Brenda and me know what you find regarding the prints. If the only prints are mine and possibly Maggie's, then I suppose the guy could have worn gloves, or accessed the bank account from somewhere else. Of course, that leaves us with the catawampus placement of my mouse."

"Who knows about the bank login issue?" Fred asked.

"Vera Fredricks," Brenda said. "She alerted Russell and me to the suspicious login this morning. Some of the employees saw you and Dani come into the building, but you're not in uniform. On the other hand, some employees know you're a detective with the police force, Fred, because you've been around asking questions about the murder."

"If anyone asks about you," Russell said, "the answer is you're updating me on the murder investigation."

"I'm good with that," Fred said. "We can't rule out the potential of an inside job."

Chapter 14

— • • • —

ANGRY BLACK CLOUDS were fast approaching Daytona Beach from the ocean. All of Florida's east coast braced for a tropical storm with winds from forty to sixty miles per hour. NOAA's nonstop weather alerts warned boaters to stay off the high seas.

Maggie put the phone call on hold and walked to the doorway of Russell's office. "Russell, Chuck's on the phone. There's trouble at the site, a sit-in of some sort. He's on line one."

"Thanks, Maggie." Russell hit the conference button so he could keep writing the report he was working on. "Chuck, what's going on?"

"Trouble, Russell. There are about a hundred protestors staging a rally at two of the entrances to the site. Someone, I think that organizer Victoria Standish, let out a blast on a bullhorn, and they all sat down in the middle of the makeshift-roads we built. I have cement trucks lined up ready to pour, and they can't get through. If they don't dump their loads soon, we'll be charged for the cement if we use it or not."

"Oh, that's just great. Much more of this and we'll have cost overruns. I'll call Manny and see if he can dispatch some patrol officers to clear the way for the trucks. Hang tight, Chuck, and don't create any confrontations. We'll let the police handle it. The demonstrators can be charged with trespassing."

— • • • —

Within ten minutes a patrol wagon and several officers arrived on the scene. The demonstrators started chanting, "No building on the beach. Keep it open for us to reach." DBPD officers arrested the woman with the bullhorn and rounded up several of the other apparent ringleaders. With the big shots in the wagon, the rest of the demonstrators moved back on their own, opening the roadway. The demonstration fizzled once the patrol wagon, carrying their leaders, left the scene.

Cement trucks drove down the cleared path following Chuck's directions to the spot prepared, ready and waiting, for the cement. After the cement was poured, Sanchez instructed his crew to leave and to return to work at the usual time tomorrow. He could see the sheets of water off in the distance. It wouldn't be long before the storm, with torrents of wind-swept rain, pelted the city.

— • • • —

Manny disconnected the call from Sanchez at the construction site. He'd called to thank Manny for his quick action and to let him know all was calm, except for the storm. Fred walked into the bullpen with hot coffee for everyone—a large for Dani. They cracked the lids to add their own cream and sugar, but not Fred. He took his black.

Taking a sip of coffee, Manny walked up to the whiteboard. His team swiveled front and center.

"Stone had a sit-in a little bit ago," Manny said. "I sent a patrol wagon over and they arrested a few ringleaders, and the demonstration immediately became a non-issue. George, question those they arrested, separately. See what you can find out. Are they just disgruntled green beans or is there more behind the rabble rousing? I also want you to assist Fred with the security interviews of Stone's inner team. You start with Fatigate and Balfor. Fred, you take Sanchez, Sitwell, and Kittles."

"No problem. I'm meeting Kittles for dinner tonight."

"Dinner?" Dani said. "Is that on or off the clock?"

"Off the clock, smarty. But whether off or on, it doesn't really concern you unless I come up with some information." He raised his eyebrows and gave Dani and George a don't-you-dare say any more stare.

"Heck, along with *the information*, I want to hear all the *he-said she-said* details from your rendezvous with the *very* attractive Miss Kittles," Dani said chuckling, ignoring Fred's warning look.

Chapter 15

—•••—

THE TROPICAL STORM was now in full force—palm trees bending as the wind whipped their long fronds, and carried debris for blocks before slamming pieces of wood, glass, or metal into the sides of buildings and fences. Ocean waves crashed on the beach, creating a powerful undertow. But some surfers pushed their luck and continued trying to catch a wave.

The DBPD wagon pulled up to the side entrance of the police department. The detainees clamored out of the van and ran into the building. The officers started processing them into holding areas. Detaining them, however briefly, gave the demonstrators a chance to cool off, and the officers a chance to question them.

George asked to have Victoria Standish brought to the interrogation room. He wanted to find out what her underlying motives were in organizing the demonstrations. Entering the room, he shut the door behind him. Victoria was slumped in a chair facing the mirrored wall. Behind the mirror, Dani stood savoring the last of the large cup of warm coffee Fred had given her.

"Hello, Miss Standish. Can I get you a cup of coffee or a soda?" George asked politely, as he sat opposite the slouched woman sucking on a cigarette.

"An ashtray would be helpful, unless you want me to flick these ashes on the floor."

George left the room, returning with a pink speckled dish. Seeing her up close, he realized she was much younger than he first assumed, perhaps in her late twenties. She was a plain girl with long brown hair tied back in a pony-tail. She wore no makeup. Her jeans and yellow T-shirt were clean, and her feet were encased in work boots.

Victoria sat up straight and looked George in the eye. "Now, about that offer of a soda. I know you want to butter me up, so I'll be real nice and agree to tell you everything. More to the point, so I'll go away and be your *vision* of a good girl?" she said, stamping out the cigarette butt in the make-do ashtray.

"I merely asked if you would like something to drink, not a psychoanalysis session, Ms. Standish. Would you like something to drink?"

"Sure, why not. I'll have a Coke with extra ice and lemon on the side, Mr.—?"

"George. Detective George Anderson. You can call me George."

Victoria rolled her eyes, shook her head, and again slouched in the chair. "Okay, George."

"Excuse me a minute while I get your soda."

"Not soda. Coke!"

George left the room again and walked down the hall to the drink machine. Dani was already there and handed him a can of Coke.

"She's a piece of work, George."

"Yes, she's a real smart ass. Maybe under that tough exterior I can find out what makes her tick." George grabbed a cup of coffee for himself and re-entered the interrogation room with Victoria's Coke.

"Sorry, we're fresh out of ice and lemon," he said, setting the can on the table.

"Figures. Hey, George, it's real hot and sticky in here. You guys forget to pay your electric bill?" Victoria asked, pulling her shirt away from her body several times to let the air circulate underneath the fabric.

"Sorry about the humidity, Ms. Standish. Sometimes with a storm, the AC can't keep up, providing its own demonstration of sorts. I'm sure you understand." George pulled a recorder out of his pants pocket and set it on the table along with a pen and a small notepad.

"George, why don't you call me Victoria? You know, seeing how we're getting all buddy-buddy."

"Is it okay with you if I tape our conversation, Victoria?"

"Sure, why not. Maybe I can convince you to stop the beach construction. You can play our little chat for all your buds."

"Maybe you can. Please give me your full name."

"Victoria Louise Standish. Never Vicki."

"Your address and telephone number, please."

"Egrets Nest Condominiums, Holly Hill. I'm in the book."

"That's a pretty nice complex. Are you employed?"

A smug smile crossed Victoria's face. She loved to blow people's minds with her address. She knew she didn't look like anybody important, maybe even homeless. "Yup. I'm the lead programmer at Schultz Software. Besides developing code for their networking program, I handle the larger installations for their accounts."

"Sounds like a very responsible position. Do they know of your, shall we say, outside activities?" George asked, wondering how this girl could possess two such opposite personas.

"Not exactly. Although the news coverage has blown my cover. Mr. Schultz, the founder of the company, is quite progressive—you know, climate-warming research and a believer in the *green* scene."

"I see. So after finding out about your demonstrations, he more or less condones your public displays?"

"You might say that," Victoria said, taking a sip out of the Coke can.

"Where did you go to school to learn to be a programmer?"

Another smirk crossed her face. "You sure want to put me down don't you, George. For your information, I have a degree in computer science from Carnegie Mellon University. You have heard of CMU haven't you?" she stated, seeming to enjoy herself.

"Yes, I have. So, Victoria, how far do you intend to carry these demonstrations? Many of the others seem to look to you for direction."

"It's a form of free speech. You can't stop us."

"That's right. However, today you were on private property, trespassing. If the owner wants to press charges, you could be arrested. In the case of a construction site, your demonstrations can cost the builders a lot of money, if your actions bring about delays. We're not going to detain you any longer, but my advice is to watch where and when you hold your gatherings. Even if you aren't on private property, if you interfere with citizens going about their daily activities, you can be arrested for disturbing the peace. Do you understand?"

"Ya, I get it. Can I go now, *George*?"

"Yes, you can go. And, Victoria, I hope I don't see you in the news again unless it's for a programmer-of-the-year award."

Chapter 16

— • • • —

BRENDA WAS STYMIED. She couldn't find any trace of the message that had been displayed on her monitor when she walked into the lab this morning. Her fingers had flown over the keyboard for hours. Her wrists ached for the first time in her life. Her head hurt, and her back was so stiff she wasn't sure she could stand up straight even if she tried. What really made her mad was that the message didn't seem to be threatening. On the other hand, the unexplained bank login was very dangerous, and she had failed to find any tracks in the system log file. The only conclusion: the intruder was a skilled programmer who didn't want to be traced.

Thankfully, her phone rang interrupting her brain's frustration. It was Fred.

"Hi, computer guru. Just thought I'd remind you of our date slash business meeting."

"Oh my. What time is it?" She looked up at her lab clock and couldn't believe the whole day was practically gone.

"It's five o'clock. I know you computer geeks, sorry, computer experts. Once you get started hunting whatever it is you're looking for, you lose all sense of time. Can you still make it at six? If not, I'll change the reservation."

"No, no, six is good. I haven't moved all day, so you've given me an excuse to leave this mushroom factory, at least for a couple of hours."

"Always glad when I can provide an excuse. At least, I think that's a good thing. Sure you don't want me to pick you up? The storm has passed, but some of the roads are a mess."

"I'm sure. See you in an hour." Brenda looked back at her monitor. She felt as if it was mocking her.

At Brenda's direction, Vera had changed all her passwords—bank account logins, and her PC. Russell had changed his passwords and Brenda had done the same—system manager login, and her PC. She had spoken with a friend at Homeland Security, who suggested she install the tracing software he had used in the past to catch a hacker.

Brenda went up to her office. She stopped in the ladies room to freshen up and ran into Catherine applying fresh lipstick.

"Brenda, what have you been doing all day in that dungeon you call a lab? I asked Sally, and she said you were trying to track something. Did you find what you were looking for?" Catherine asked.

"Yes, I was in the mushroom factory most of the day, and no, I didn't find what I was looking for. My back hurts and I feel a doozy of a headache coming on. Other than that, everything is peachy-keen." Even though she was irritated, a smile managed to cross her face. "By the way, I called Lucy earlier. I won't be able to have dinner with you two tonight."

"Oh, a big date?"

"No, it is *not* a date. It's a business meeting with Detective Watson."

"Ah. Sounds like a date to me with a little funny business thrown in." Catherine chided, with a smile.

"Well, I prefer to think of it as *all* business. I don't date."

"Okay, okay. Have fun. In the future, after you move in, do you want me to wait up for you?"

"Very funny, mother. Speaking about moving in, I'm glad I saw you. Is it okay if I bring my meager belongings over tomorrow after work? I may have to make more than one trip. If I start Friday, I can finish Saturday morning. I'm looking forward to my first night in my beautiful new room."

"You bring your things over anytime. You have the key and the run of the house."

"Terrific, and thanks again, Catherine," Brenda said, giving Catherine a hug. "Now, if you'll excuse me, I'm going to finish freshening up and leave for my *business* meeting."

—•••—

Fred arrived at the Aquarium restaurant a little early and managed to grab a corner table on the deck looking out over the Halifax River. The storm was long gone, and the air was fresh but warm and quite humid. As usual, the Aquarium provided a unique ambiance with several large glass tanks, creating room dividers, a home to exotic colored fish swimming in and out of greenery and various rock formations. The bar was outlined with blue neon tube lights. The columns behind the bar were accented with the lights running floor to ceiling with pink and blue neon. The waiter came over with a glass of ice water and a lemon wedge perched on the side.

"Would you like to order, sir?"

"Not yet. I'm waiting for another party. Tell you what you can do, however, please bring me two extra-dry martinis with olives. Oh, and make sure they're ice cold. Thanks."

The waiter returned with the drinks Fred ordered just as Brenda made her way to the table. Fred quickly rose to greet her.

"Hey there. Right on time." He moved to hold her chair.

"Fred, I'm a big girl. I can manage a chair, thank you."

"Okay. Just trying to be thoughtful. I was raised to hold a chair for a lady, especially a pretty lady," Fred said. *This isn't a good start,* he thought. "You sounded beat on the phone. I took the liberty of ordering you a drink. If you don't want a martini, or if you prefer something else, I'll send it back."

"Actually, it's the best thing I've seen all day. Thank you, and I'm sorry if I sounded rude. This is lovely on the river. How far are we from the ocean, less than a mile?"

"That's about right, far enough you don't get the beach traffic, but close enough to feel the air off the ocean. I take it you didn't find the origin of the message this morning," Fred said.

"No, I didn't. It's not so much the message, which certainly seemed harmless, but why is there no entry in the email log, or better yet, the system log file?"

"Maybe it was just a quirky thing," Fred suggested, trying to ease her mind.

"Fred, quirky things don't happen on a computer. There is always a cause and effect. Finding the cause can sometimes be a real puzzle. But the really bad event is the unexplained bank login. I didn't find an answer to that either. Again, the tracks were virtually swept away. Did Dani come up with any mystery prints on Russell's desk or mouse?"

"Not yet, but I'll find out more from her tomorrow morning."

"Jack Fatigate stopped in the lab. He hoped I wasn't going to bring the system down again. He wasn't happy that he only had a few seconds notice. Have you talked to him yet?"

"No. I decided to start with the head of computer security. I believe her name is Miss Kittles," Fred said, with a smile and a quick wink.

The waiter approached Fred's table and asked if they would like to order. Brenda gave him her order for pasta Alfredo, with shrimp on the side. Fred decided on a ten-ounce sirloin steak. "Can you smother that with mushrooms?" he asked. The waiter made a note on his pad.

"Brenda, would you like a glass of wine with dinner?" Fred asked, looking into her dark brown eyes.

"You know what? I'd like another martini," she said to the waiter.

"Make that two martinis, and please don't rush the entrees," Fred added, handing the waiter their menus. *I want this evening to last a while,* he thought.

"I'm glad you didn't slip home and change—you look good in all black," Brenda said with a smile. "What to wear here is such a problem for me. It's cool in the morning, so my pantsuits are perfect, and of course my lab is ice cold, but then in the afternoon I'd love to change into shorts."

"Now, that I'd like to see." Fred leaned forward in his chair, taking a sip of his drink. He wanted to know more about this dynamic woman. She was definitely dedicated to her job. But she wasn't forth coming with any personal information. *I don't want to pry. Maybe if I approach her slowly. Ask some off-hand, harmless questions.*

"Where are you from, Brenda? I don't recognize an accent."

"My family lives in Alaska...Juneau, where I grew up."

"That's about as far away from Florida as you can get," Fred said, leaning back in his chair.

"In high school, I became intrigued with computers. A year before graduation I applied to Carnegie Mellon University. Wonder of wonders, they accepted my application in their computer science program."

"So that's where you learned all that *geeky*, excuse me, techi stuff."

"What I found out was that all that *geeky* stuff wasn't enough. But, Homeland Security hired me as a rookie—accompanying agents on their assignments, so I could learn the ropes."

"Sounds tough, especially after you had all that computer training."

"Well, like many dreams, the reality of a situation doesn't always match the vision. Airplanes quickly became my home. To say the least, I wasn't thrilled. When I saw the ad that Stone & Associates was looking for a head of computer security, I jumped at it."

"That's quite a journey you've made—Alaska, Washington DC, and now Florida, with points in between. Quite a different climate—Alaska and Florida. How do you like it here?"

Their dinner arrived putting the conversation on hold as the waiter placed the piping hot plates on the table along with the martinis. He also lit the single votive in the center of the table, creating an intimate atmosphere as the sun set.

"Anything else I can get for you folks?"

"No, this will be fine for now," they said in unison, looking up at the waiter.

"Sorry, I didn't mean to speak for you," Fred said. "I just—"

"It's quite all right. No problem, really."

Both were hungry and immediately dove into their dinners. Brenda picked up the conversation with the question Fred had asked.

"I like Florida a lot. There's so much *day* time, not like the long nights in Alaska. The heat, however, takes some getting used to." Brenda took a sip of her martini, sat back in her chair, and looked at Fred, as if for the first time. "How about you, Fred? Where do you hail from?"

"Santa Fe, New Mexico. Before illegal immigration grabbed the spotlight, drugs coming over the border were already a big problem. I decided early on, like you, to go into law enforcement. Manny recruited me from Santa Fe because of my record in apprehending illegals."

"How did you get that scar on your face?"

"Let's just say my size helped to intimidate frightened people crossing the border. However, this scar across my cheek clearly shows that not all were impressed," Fred said, as his fingers traced the scar tissue. "Brenda, can I ask you a couple of questions about the access to your lab?"

"Ah, yes. The business meeting part of our dinner," she said smiling. "Access is gained only by knowing the code for the keypad on the door. Unless, of course, you push the buzzer, like you did this morning. If I'm there, and want to let the person in, I press a lock-release button on my side of the door."

"Who knows the access code?"

"Our building security director, Ben Sitwell, as we learned when he showed us his logbook this morning. My assistant, Sally, knows the code, as do Russell and Catherine. I don't know about anyone else, except maybe Vera, the CFO. Oh, wait a minute, Vera came into the lab this morning without buzzing."

"And how about your office on the third floor?"

"Same thing. However, when I'm in my office I generally leave the door open. Russell likes an open-door policy. Excuse me just a moment. The breeze is so refreshing. This weather is such a change from the violence of that storm earlier." Brenda closed her eyes, savoring the soft tropical air.

"Just one of the perks of living in Daytona Beach, my dear."

"Okay, I've had my moment. You were saying?"

"When you arrived at work, the morning the cleaner was murdered, did you notice anyone, or anything different?" Fred asked.

"Not until after the groundbreaking. When the van pulled into the parking lot, there were three of your squad cars by the dumpster with their lights flashing. I had to walk past them because I use that side door if I'm not going straight up to my office," Brenda said.

"Did anybody tell you what happened?"

"No, and I didn't ask. The officers all seemed pretty busy. Russell had scheduled our first staff meeting, and he told us as we left the van, that he would find out what all the commotion was about."

"Who was at the staff meeting?"

"All of the people who report directly to Russell, except Sanchez. He was still at the site. The groundbreaking was the first time we were all together. We were excited about getting the development started."

"You mean you hadn't met all of them before that day?"

"That's right, well actually the only one I hadn't met was Chuck Sanchez. He spends almost all of his time at the site."

"What do you think of the others?"

"I've talked to Ben Sitwell a couple of times. He only uses his computer for email, a few spreadsheets, and occasionally some word processing. We don't have much interaction because he's in charge of building security, you know the bricks and mortar, while I'm responsible for the virtual security of the company—the bits and bytes. And, of course, the computers."

"How about the other two men?"

"You mean Balfor and Fatigate?"

"Yes. They're VPs aren't they?"

"It seems to me everyone is a VP. I enjoy working with both of them. They're the only two who have a clue about what is going on at the other end of their mouse. Both of them are very computer savvy. Balfor has to be in order to keep his project software running smoothly. All the departments dump information into his program. He then stirs it all together and pours much of it into Fatigate's purchasing software, which in turn spits out a list of what is needed at the time. He then buys all the stuff to keep the construction going. Fatigate has to understand fully how the project software interfaces with his purchasing program, so he can see if something is amiss."

"Sounds complex."

"It actually works very well, so long as I keep the roads open?"

"Excuse me, the roads?"

"The *network*, detective. All the super highways and little byways on which information travels," Brenda said, laughing.

Over dinner Fred relaxed and sensed that Brenda also let her wall down a little. He didn't understand why she had been so standoffish in the lab, but he was glad to see a crack in her armor. The two chatted more about places they had worked, as well as good and bad employers along the way. Fred flagged the waiter and asked him to bring a couple of espressos. Of course, he checked first with Brenda to be sure she wanted an after-dinner coffee.

It was now dark outside, and the reflection of the causeway lights spanning the river from the mainland to the beach side were caught twinkling on the water. In the distance, the window lights from the high-rise condominiums along the waterfront added their festive sparkle, blending with the night sky filled with stars. The waiter came over and laid the check folder on the table by Fred. Brenda reached over, opened the folder, promptly pulled out her wallet and laid several bills down.

"Now, young lady," Fred said, "what do you think you're doing? I invited *you*, remember?"

"*Detective*, this is a business meeting. *Remember?* I'll pay for my own dinner."

"Okay, I won't cause a scene provided you'll have dinner with me again as a date. I've enjoyed being with you this evening, and I'd like to see you again. *Unofficially.* Is that a deal, or am I going to have to call the waiter over here and make a scene with a request for two checks?"

"Fred, stop making a fuss. Yes, we'll call it a deal, on one condition."

"And what is that?"

"Don't you dare get up and help poor little old me out of my chair," she said, giving him an, *I dare you* wide-eyed stare.

Chapter 17

—•••—

"HEY, PEACHES, cut that out. I almost spilled my morning nerve zapper," Dani said, holding onto her cup as her arm swung up in the air. "I know, I know, you want a biscuit. Tell your master to stop scowling, because I'm going to give you one anyway," she said, fishing out a treat in the shape of a medium-sized bone from her bottom desk drawer.

Peaches gently took the treat from Dani's delicate fingers and flopped down on her pillow next to Manny's desk. She first licked the tasty morsel, then bit off the end. Her ears were back, eyes half closed, as she savored the treat.

"Dani..." Manny said, cocking his head to the side.

"I know, but she said please. So what am I suppose to do, looking into those big brown eyes? Say, no? I don't think so."

Manny looked down at his pooch. "You're spoiled rotten, you know."

Peaches answered with one thump of her tail, swallowing the last piece of the biscuit.

"All right everyone, let's see where we are with the Stone case. If we don't start getting some answers, we'll all be assigned to cleaning out the cells. Fred, any leads on the murder victim?"

"No. I've had a couple of sessions with Ben Sitwell, the head of building security. There are no cameras on the outside of the building, but there is a camera in the lobby. Sitwell said he personally viewed the pictures but didn't see anything suspicious. He gave me copies on a flash drive, which I have right here." Fred picked up a light-brown envelope from the corner of his desk and handed it to Dani.

"So, he said he didn't see anything out of the ordinary?" Dani asked.

"That's right, but I'd like you to take a look at the files, Dani. Unfortunately, there are several employees who use the side door, because it's closer to the employee parking lot. No camera on that door. So, no record. In talking to the cleaner's family, friends, and co-workers, they all say the same thing—he was well liked, didn't have any enemies, and no one can imagine how anything so terrible could happen to such a nice guy."

"Yes, well, we'll see," Manny said. "George, what happened at the construction site? Damn storm was enough of a hindrance without the added nuisance of a sit-in."

"I did have a chat with Miss Standish."

"What's her story?" Fred asked.

"She's definitely a conflicted young woman," George said. "On the one hand, she's a computer professional with a degree in Computer Science from Carnegie Mellon University. On the other hand, she's this flower child who wants to save the planet, and in particular, our beaches from unwanted encroachment."

"Well now, that's interesting," Fred said, taking a swig from his bottle of water. "That's two times in the last twenty-four hours I've heard about Carnegie Mellon University."

"What's the other one?" Manny asked.

"From Brenda Kittles during dinner last night."

"Whoa, partner. How was your dinner with the lovely Miss Kittles?" Dani asked, sitting up straight, her right hand over her heart.

"Miss Trotter, as I told you before, this was a business meeting...of sorts," Fred replied, knowing he was in for some class-A ribbing.

"Ah, give, Fred. Just explain to me the *sorts,* if you please," Dani said sighing.

"We discussed what she observed the morning of the murder, smarty pants. Anyway, she too has a degree from Carnegie Mellon, specializing in computer forensics. She's a few years older than Standish, so I doubt they ever met."

"That makes three women we men better hope never get together—Kittles, Standish, and Dani here. Can you imagine that conversation?" Manny chuckled.

"There's more," Fred said. "Dani and I were called back to Russell's office. A login had occurred into the corporate bank account at 3:12 and a logout at 3:14, and it was attributed to Mr. Stone."

"So—" George said.

"So, it was 3:12 a.m. and he was home in bed. Brenda had an idea that someone may have used Stone's computer—I guess a computer leaves a unique ID when performing some operations."

"It sure does," Dani said, tossing her empty coffee container into the wastebasket.

"Anyway, Dani dusted the office for prints."

"I only found Mr. Stone's and Ms. O'Reilly's, his assistant," Dani said.

"I do have a beginning of a theory," Fred said. "For conversation purposes, let's say someone wanted access to their computer system. The perpetrator kills the cleaner for his keys and enters the building. Ben's office is just to the right of that side door. His nameplate reads, Ben Sitwell, Building Security, and the door is unlocked because his keypad is malfunctioning. The bad guy then goes to the computer lab and sees that it requires an access code. He, we'll use the male gender until we have reason to change it, goes back to Ben's office, sees the notebook with *codes* on the spine."

"Yes, and—?" Manny asked.

"That's it for now."

"Thing is, an outsider would have to know the user ID and password to login to the bank account," Dani said.

"Okay, but an insider, might know how to get to the information," George volunteered.

"The bank login could be a dry run," Manny said. "A test to get at the millions of dollars that will soon be deposited into S&A's bank account."

Chapter 18

—•••—

BRENDA OPENED HER car's sunroof, breathing in the fresh air flowing through with the change in the weather—yesterday dark and sinister, today sunny, hot and humid with a thirty percent chance of rain in the afternoon. It was a typical summer weather pattern for the mid-coast of Florida. As Brenda entered her office, Sally noticed a new spring in her step, and a smile had replaced yesterday's perplexed frown.

"TGIF, boss," Sally said, following Brenda into her office. "A couple of telephone calls came in over the past hour. None look urgent, but Detective Watson said to tell you thanks. He wouldn't say for what. Can I get you anything?"

"TGIF it is, Sally, and no I don't need anything. I'm going down to the lab in a few minutes. Come to think of it, there is one thing you can do for me. I'm moving in with Catherine Hainsworth."

"Wonderful! That's really cool, I like her a lot."

"Yes, it is *cool*. Will you see that my personnel file is updated? Let me know if they need me to sign anything. Be sure to note my cell phone as the contact number."

"When will this be effective?" Sally asked.

"Tonight. I don't have much to move, so I should be able to clean out my rental by tomorrow sometime."

Brenda picked up her messages and headed down to the lab. Outside the lab door she punched in her code. At the click of the lock release, she stepped inside. She reached for the light switch, but, before she flicked the lights on, she noticed her monitor glowed with a different desktop image. There were words in very small characters on the screen. She couldn't decipher what it said from the door, so she drew closer to read the fine print.

> *"Hello, Brenda.*
>
> *I told you I would return with rules for our little game. I love games, don't you? In case you don't know the game of chess, I will help you. The purpose of the game is to trap your opponent's king, to get him in such a position that he is helpless, he can't move. When your king is trapped, Brenda, I will win and you will lose. Next time I will begin to let you know how the different chess pieces change position. Until then, goodbye."*

The dark red words seemed to float over what appeared to be a chess board with gray and white squares—the pawn in front of the black king had been moved forward two squares. Brenda knew this was sometimes the first move in a chess game. A game she did not want to play.

Brenda noted that her shortcuts, and other icons, were in their usual places on her monitor's desktop. She walked back to the door and flicked on the light switch. Returning to her desk, she put her hand on her mouse. Clicking the mouse button on the right side, she selected the word "Properties" from the menu that popped up on her screen. From the tabs along the top of the "Display Properties" dialog box, she selected the "Desktop" tab. The setting for the current desktop was *ChessGame*.

"Damn it. How did you get in the lab? If you came in through the network, then how did you get into my space on the server? I don't know who you are, but I will win this game. I will find you," she whispered, through clenched teeth.

Her telephone rang and she snatched the receiver. "Kittles," she answered still seething from the setting on her screen.

"Brenda, this is Russell. Are you okay? You sound upset."

"Hi, Russell. I'm okay...well, actually, I'm mad. But you called me. What can I do for you?"

"Catherine just stopped by and told me you accepted her offer to stay with her for a while. Personally, I'm glad you are. I think it will be a good thing for both of you."

"I do too. I still can't believe she invited me. Russell, I have to change the subject. Can you come down to the lab a minute? I want to show you something."

"Sure. I'll be right down."

Brenda hung-up the phone and suddenly had an idea where she might find the first message. She again clicked the button on the right side of her mouse and followed the same path she took before, selecting "Properties" on the pop-up menu. But this time from the Display Properties dialog box she selected the tab labeled "Screen Saver." The screen saver setting was "DaVinci," the one she generally selected. Scrolling down the list of screen-saver choices, she found what she was looking for. In alphabetical order, there was a screen saver named *GoodMorningBrenda*. Checking further, she found that an executable command for a sound was embedded in the screen-saver file. She double-clicked the command and a faint laugh, the same one she heard the first time, emanated from her speakers.

"I'm so stupid not to think of this," she said, slapping her head. "No wonder I couldn't print it. The instant I touched my mouse, the screen saver automatically disappeared and the sound command was triggered."

She heard the click indicating someone punched in the code to open her door. Slightly on edge, she whirled around just as Russell entered the lab.

"Russell, I'm so glad you called. Let me show you something."

Brenda turned back to her monitor. She opened the "Screen Saver" box, and clicked "Preview."

The screen saver displayed the message: *"Good morning, Brenda. I'll return soon—"* Brenda quickly jiggled her mouse to remove the screen saver, and Russell heard the faint laugh.

"Is this how you greet yourself in the morning?" Russell asked, with a chuckle.

"Russell, I did not type this message. I have something else to show you."

Again, with her fingers positioned over her mouse, she brought up the desktop file Chess*Game* and clicked the *Preview* button.

Squinting, Russell leaned over her shoulder so he could read the fine print. "What do you make of this?" he asked.

"I don't know what to make of it. Other than, I sure don't like it. Someone is getting into our system and playing some practical jokes, only I'm not laughing. This monitor is connected directly to the server computer. In order to get to my working area, I have to login with my user ID and password. If a prankster is playing games, I'm going to put a stop to it."

—•••—

Brenda opened her logbook to enter the latest event. After noting the date, she wrote: "Friday, 9:10 a.m. Someone accessed my computer account and added a desktop file, *ChessGame*. I also located the previous message of a week ago, which was added to the screen saver choices: *GoodMorningBrenda*. I showed both to Russell Stone."

Two hours later, she made another entry: "Friday, 11:35 a.m. Assumption: an unauthorized person accessed the system user ID and password file. He could now login as System Manager, the highest level of privilege—access to everything on the system, and erase all signs of ever having been in there. Any trace of someone copying or loading the above listed files to my computer did not appear in the system log file. The prankster swept away his footprints."

Chapter 19

—•••—

"BAD BAD DAY TO MOVE," Brenda said to her image in the rearview mirror, as she pulled out of the company's parking lot. She had checked the security protocols again, plugged holes where an intruder might gain entrance, and changed the user ID's and passwords one more time. After entering these steps in her logbook, she turned off the lights, left the building, and headed to her rental apartment.

Arriving in just under ten minutes, Brenda hurriedly stuffed the first load of her belongings in her car, and was now on her way to Catherine's, albeit a little over the speed limit. "If Fred catches me speeding, he'll probably throw me in the clink," she muttered. "It may not be a good day to move, but then what day is."

The late afternoon air seemed more stifling than usual. The temperature was down a few degrees from its high of ninety-seven, but the humidity hadn't dissipated at all. *Welcome to paradise in August,* she thought, turning the AC on high and directing the vents to blast cold air in her face. Her mind was setting up a tactical list of procedures she had to make to prohibit the prankster from accessing her system again. The work she had done this morning was a good start, but not enough.

She needed to check if there were traces of a rat coming through the network cable. She planned to trace the culprit back to his computer. "Why do we always assume the male gender? The prankster could just as easily be female. Well, I can just see Vera frolicking through the pipeline. Not! From now on, I'll call him ChessMan. Oh God, there may be more than one—a group," she said to her nonexistent passenger, slapping the steering wheel in frustration.

Coming to Catherine's driveway, Brenda backed up as close as she could get to the front door. Popping the hatch of her cream-colored PT Cruiser, she reached in filling her arms with clothes. Lucy opened the front door and hustled down the three steps to help her.

"Here, Miss Brenda, let me take some of those clothes."

"Oh, Lucy, bless you. Thanks for keeping a lookout for me. Let's just dump them on the bed. I'll put everything away later."

Lucy followed Brenda to her bedroom. They both placed their loads on top of the bed and headed out for another armful. They almost collided with Catherine coming down the hall.

"Hey, you two, looks like moving day," she said happy to see Brenda had started her move. "Can I help?"

"You can be the boss. Let us know if anything is dragging," Brenda called out over her shoulder, as she stuck her head into the car to retrieve the remaining items. "Because of Lucy, I think this is the end of it for now. Catherine, can you close the hatch? Lucy and I will dump these clothes, and then I, for one, will be ready for a glass of wine."

"You got it," Catherine said, closing Brenda's hatchback and all the open car doors. She headed into the house and back to the kitchen. After pouring a glass of iced tea, she retrieved a bottle of chardonnay from the refrigerator, just as Lucy and Brenda joined her.

"What would you like, Brenda, red or white?"

"That bottle of chardonnay in your hand looks icy cold and perfect for a day like today. I have to admit I'm tempted to fly back to Alaska. How long is it going to stay this way?" she asked, picking up her wine glass, raising it to her friends, and taking a sip of the very cold golden liquid.

"The weather report said the heat wave is going to be with us for at least one, possibly two, more weeks. Your first summer will be the hardest. After that you'll know what to expect, and you simply plan for it." Catherine replied. "Lucy, would you like red or white wine?"

"Oh, Miss Catherine, I don't know. I really don't drink much."

"Come on Lucy, this is a big day. I'm having iced tea, would you prefer that or will you take me up on the wine?"

"Well, it is hot. I guess I'll try the same as Miss Brenda, but just a half a glass."

Catherine poured Lucy a little wine and handed it to her. "Here's to my two new roommates. May many happy days lay ahead for the three of us."

"Here here, I'll drink to that," Brenda said.

The three women taped each other's glasses and headed for the kitchen table.

"I know you've had a tough day at work, Brenda, on top of moving. How many more trips before you're finished?" Catherine asked.

"I figure three or four. As I said, I don't really have much except my clothes. The place was furnished complete with pots and pans. I'm not going back tonight, but I do want to get a jump on it in the morning. My plan is to finish tomorrow before noon and then head back to my lab. By that time my game plan on how to find my intruder should be fleshed out, in my head anyway."

"Dinner will take me only a few minutes," Lucy said. "I wasn't sure what time you two wanted to eat tonight so I made a pan of lasagna this morning. I can heat it up in the microwave real quick like. A Caesar salad is ready in the refrigerator."

"Lucy, you are a woman after my heart. I'm feeling like the luckiest person in the world to have hooked up with you two girls."

"It's much too hot to fuss," Catherine said. "Let's have dinner together in the kitchen."

"I love your kitchen, Catherine," Brenda said. "It's so open yet homey. Would you call it a Spanish influence? The colors are so vibrant—deep yellow with reds, and greens, and I see splashes of purple and pale blue."

"I melded the Mediterranean and Caribbean influences together, except for the cabinets. I didn't want oak or pine. The cherry wood has a light stain so the grain shows through. I did splurge on the copper hood over the stove."

"And, I love this round glass table in the bay window with a view of your garden. I can see a highchair with a little one peeking out at that bird feeder."

Turning away from the window, Catherine said, "Tomorrow, Manny's coming over to take a look at the guns Peter kept in the safe. I told him that I felt rather vulnerable, and I wanted to have a gun available to protect myself." She paused noting the surprised look on Lucy's face.

"I think that's a good idea," Brenda said. "Maybe it's because of my previous job with Homeland Security, or just living in a big city, I always have a small revolver in my desk at work."

"Do you keep it loaded?" Catherine asked.

"Yes, but it's somewhat hidden under a black cloth, so if someone is standing beside me when I open the drawer to get a pen or something, they don't freak out."

"My, you modern women. But I can understand why you want a gun for protection, Miss Catherine."

Chapter 20

—•••—

SATURDAY MORNING shoppers were sweating in the muggy haze and eighty-nine degree temperature. The forecast called for the afternoon high of close to a hundred. The storm long gone, Catherine's gardener arrived early to pick up the debris littering the lawn—palm fronds and broken branches.

In an effort to help Lucy with her new routine, Catherine suggested that they each get their own breakfast except on Sunday. Lucy insisted on fixing Sunday breakfast with her thick, but fluffy, buttermilk waffles. Being as she was likely to be the first one up, she would also put on the coffee. Then it was everyone for herself. Lucy put a magnetic pad on the refrigerator for groceries items that Catherine and Brenda would like her to purchase the next time out.

Today, however, everyone seemed to congregate at the same time for their first morning together. Brenda, dressed in black Capri's and a light tan T-shirt, poured her coffee, retrieved some cereal from the cupboard, and a banana from the fruit basket. Lucy was already at the table writing her to-do list when Catherine wandered in, dressed for Saturday errands in jeans, white T-shirt, and black sandals. Her blonde hair was held back with a red ribbon.

"You two are a beautiful sight to see this morning," Catherine said, pouring a glass of milk. "Lucy, how soon do you think you'll be able to move in permanently?"

"In about three weeks, Miss Catherine. I've moved most of my clothes, and as you can see, I slept here last night. I didn't want to miss our first morning together. I'm moving a few things into storage and plan to have a yard sale for everything else next weekend."

"Can I help you," both Brenda and Catherine said at the same time, laughing at each other.

"Thank you very much, ladies, but you both have enough goin' on with your work. I wouldn't dream of asking you. A couple of my neighbors have offered to help, so I think I'm covered."

The doorbell rang and Lucy went to answer it.

"Captain Manny, and Peaches. Good morning." Peaches muscled her way through the door, sat in front of Lucy, and put a paw up on her white bib-apron. "Yes, you're a good dog. My, she certainly seems to feel at home." Peaches trotted off to the kitchen to find Catherine.

"Seems that dog of yours has a nose for food, captain."

"Always has, Lucy. Always has. Hello, what do we have here, a coffee klatch?"

"Hello, Manny," Catherine said, rising to give him a hug. "Have you met Brenda Kittles."

"Yes, I have. Hello, Brenda. I heard you were moving in with Cat. A wonderful idea. Someone needs to keep an eye on this lady."

"How about a cup of coffee, captain?" Lucy asked.

"Thank you, Lucy, I believe I will."

"Captain Salinas—" Brenda started to say.

"Please, call me Manny."

"Manny. I'm glad you're helping to pick out a weapon for Catherine. I'll be interested to see what you and Catherine choose."

"Do you think you might have a need at work, Brenda?" Manny asked, taking a sip of coffee.

"I told Catherine that I keep a revolver in my desk drawer in the lab. When I was with Homeland Security, I almost always carried a weapon. But to answer your question, there've been a couple of unusual events on our computer system, and I'm feeling just a little uneasy."

"I can see you're concerned," Manny said.

"Well, enough of this wonderful interlude, folks," Brenda said. "I have to be on my way, if I'm going to reach my goal to move the rest of my stuff by noon. Don't plan any meals for me, Lucy. I'll be going to work after that, so I don't know when I'll be home. Home! What a wonderful word."

Brenda rinsed her dishes, put them in the dishwasher, and then she walked over to Catherine. "Thanks again, Catherine," she said, leaning over and giving Catherine a quick hug. "By the way, I like Manny's nickname for you. Do you mind if I call you Cat?"

"Please do. No matter what time you get in, give a rap on my door, so we can fill each other in on what we did today." Catherine said, giving Brenda a wink. "She's like having a sister in the house," she said to Manny.

"Will do. Bye all. Lucy, good luck with your packing."

"Manny, how about you and I take our coffee into the library and check out those guns."

"Okay. Thanks for the coffee, Lucy."

"No problem, captain. Miss Catherine, I'll be on my way as well."

Peaches followed her master into the library.

— ••• —

Catherine opened the safe and retrieved two wooden boxes. Each box contained two guns wrapped in a tan, soft-flannel cloth. Manny carefully unwrapped the guns, laying them on the cherry coffee table.

"This is quite a collection, Cat. But, they're all quite heavy, almost two pounds each or more. The revolver I have in mind for you weighs less than a pound. Here, you pick up each one so you can feel the heft," Manny said, handing her one of the guns.

"Yes. I see what you mean by heft."

"I'll wrap them back up, and then let's head to the gun shop. Okay with you?"

— ••• —

Manny pulled out of Catherine's driveway and headed for the department to drop Peaches off. It was much too hot to leave her for any length of time in the car. Besides, he wanted to see Fred, if he was in, or give him a call. Manny didn't like Brenda's body language. Something was bothering her, and he thought Fred might be able to help ease her mind, to let her know she wasn't alone in tackling the problem.

It only took a few minutes for Manny to take Peaches up to the bullpen and to give Fred a heads-up about Brenda. He rejoined Catherine in the car and they headed over to Buck's Gun Rack.

"This is some car you have, captain. All these gadgets blinking and squawking at you."

"All part of the territory, Cat," he said, looking over at her. *This is nice,* he thought, *having her sit beside me on Saturday morning, running errands.*

Manny parked the car in front of the shop, where a life-size wooden Indian sat by the front door. As they passed the replica, the Indian raised his arm and beat the drum held in his lap three times. Entering the busy shop, several salespeople greeted Manny as well as Buck Jr., the son of the man who founded the shop in 1954. Manny asked to see two of the Smith & Wesson revolvers.

"Here, Cat, hold this one. How does it feel?" Manny asked, placing the revolver in her hand.

Catherine lifted the gun up and down a few times. "When will I be able to pick it up?"

"There's a three-day waiting period so probably by next Wednesday. When you have the gun, we'll go out to the range a couple of times so you get the hang of firing it."

"Sounds good, captain. Do you think they'll consider me a risky person given I've been taken hostage twice?" she whispered in jest.

"No. I'd say you're a perfect candidate to carry a small handgun for protection. No bad guy is going to mess with you, Cat. I guarantee you," he said solemnly.

Chapter 21

— • • • —

BRENDA CHANGED HER MIND. Turning left instead of right she headed for her lab. She'd get the balance of her things from her rental apartment later. Right now she wanted to pursue some ideas she had during the night on how to trace the intruder. She parked her PT Cruiser and headed for the side entrance. Opening the door, she ran smack into Ben Sitwell.

"Ben, what are you doing here on a Saturday morning?"

"I might ask the same of you, Brenda."

She didn't see the man standing behind Ben. Ben moved aside to let her pass and she bumped into the stranger.

"Sorry," she said. "I seem to be playing dodgem this morning."

"Brenda, this man is a locksmith. He's changing the locks on all the outside doors except for the main entrance. Russell wants everyone to come in through the lobby for a while."

"Oh, that'll be convenient. Not."

"I know. I know. There'll be a crash bar in case of a fire. Come on in," Ben said, "but Monday morning you'll have to come in the front of the building. Also, when you leave today, you'll have to go out through the lobby, unless you want to set off the alarm," Ben said with a chuckle.

"If you say so, Ben. See you later."

Brenda went on down the hall, punched in the code to her lab and entered. She flicked on the lights, and with a little apprehension looked over at her monitor. No messages.

After an hour of leaning over her keyboard, she straightened up and decided to get a cold drink. Leaving the lab she went to the nearest beverage machine by the back entrance. Ben and the lock guy had left. She put the coins in the machine, retrieved the bottle of soda and headed back to the lab. Hesitating, she turned around to see if the crash bar had been installed. It was just as Ben said it would be. "This is going to be so unhandy," she muttered, retracing her steps to the lab to resume her work.

A short while later she was startled by the sound of the lab door buzzer. Irritated, she turned to see who it was and saw Fred, hands in the air, signaling that he was sorry for the intrusion.

"Okay, I'm coming." She smiled in spite of herself as she walked over to let him in. He was such a big guy to have such a sheepish look on his face. A pale yellow golf shirt was drawn tight over his biceps adding to his massive appearance, but his grin immediately gave him away as being one of the good guys.

"Don't tell me. Manny called you. Am I right?" Brenda asked.

"Guilty as charged, ma'am. After you talked to him this morning, he asked me to look in on you. He told me you were going to be in the lab later, but I took a chance to see if your car was in the parking lot."

"Quite the detective, aren't you. I suppose you mentioned to him that you already knew about my dilemma?"

"Gee, it totally slipped my mind. Honestly though, he wanted you to know the team is here to help. How are you coming with your own investigation? Find anything?"

"Unfortunately, no. I've gone over the system logs, but nothing unusual popped out. It's like when somebody walks in the snow, and then they retrace their steps, placing their feet in the exact same spot as they retreat. But, while retreating, they also whisk the snow back and forth obliterating their tracks. Well, that's how it looks in my system log, as if whoever was here brushed away his tracks as he retreated."

"Are you planning to spend the day here, or, as I was told, are you going to finish your move?"

"I think I'll take door number two and leave. I've tried the ideas I had during the night, so now I'm just spinning my wheels."

"Can I offer a suggestion?"

"What do you have in mind?" she asked, looking at him suspiciously.

"Not a date, Kittles, just a friend offering to help you move. My jeep isn't very big, but it holds more than you think."

"What, no squad car? No whirling lights?"

"Funny. Very funny. What do you say? We'll get you moved and then grab a bite to eat and maybe a drink to wash it down."

"Okay, *friend*, but we go Dutch treat."

"You're a hard woman, Kittles, but Dutch it is. Let's get out of this mushroom factory."

"Hey, watch your mouth, Watson. I can call my lab that, but I take offense if someone else does. This *mushroom factory*, as you call it, happens to contain the heart and soul of Stone & Associates." Smiling, she flicked off the lights as they left the lab. "We have to go out the main entrance. The locks were changed this morning, so we can't come in or go out the side door anymore."

— • • • —

Over the next four hours, Brenda and Fred loaded both of their cars and made two rounds trips to Catherine's house. Brenda was surprised at how much stuff she had accumulated, and, if truth be told, she was glad to have Fred's help. Of course, she had to take time to vacuum and to clean out the refrigerator. During this part of the operation, Fred settled on the couch and watched the time trials for the NASCAR race later in the day.

Finally finished with the cleaning chores, they headed to Catherine's. It didn't take them long to empty their cars. Depositing the last load of her belongings in her new room, they headed out in Fred's jeep to get something to eat. Neither Catherine, nor Lucy was home.

"Where are we going to dine, detective? I'm famished."

"Have you been to the North Turn, over on the beach side?"

"No. Just tell me they have food and ice cold beer. I'm generally not a beer drinker, but it's so hot today, an icy beer sounds very appealing."

"You got it, lady. One ice cold beer coming up."

Fred's little red Jeep Wrangler, windows down, roof open, sped over the causeway. Brenda enjoyed the breeze the open car afforded her and leaned her head back on the headrest.

"I can truthfully say this is the best I've felt all day, except for my morning coffee with Cat and Lucy."

"Ah, I see you've picked up on Manny's pet name for Catherine. He's the only one I know, except now you, who calls her Cat. She's such a sophisticated lady that Catherine really suits her."

"She's the best. After I heard Manny address her as Cat, I asked her if she minded if I did the same. I have a feeling we'll become very close friends."

Fred looked over at the beautiful woman sitting next to him. *I wish we could become close friends,* he thought. The few times he'd been with her, he'd felt his pulse quicken, a sensation that only happened a couple of times over the last few years. He, like Brenda, had buried himself in his work. There just hadn't been an opportunity to pursue a personal life, or maybe it was because he hadn't met a woman he wanted to pursue. Brenda was different— he wanted to spend more time with her. He enjoyed her company. If only he could break down the barrier she seemed to hide behind. He pulled into the beach parking lot across the street from the restaurant. It was late afternoon and the restaurant's parking lot was full, but the lot for beach goers still had a few spots.

"Looks like a popular place," Brenda said, getting out of the car as Fred came around to her side.

"It is, especially on a hot day like today. You'll see why in a minute."

They entered into a dark hallway, but Brenda could see a bar ahead and the ocean beyond that. Her eyes adjusted from the bright sunlight as they entered the bar. Fred steered her out the large sliding glass doors onto the patio dotted with several colorful umbrella tables. The deck was a lovely spot, and she immediately could see why the parking lot was so full.

Fred headed to a table at the front edge of the patio which looked down on the sandy beach. There was a break in the railing with steps leading down to the water. The tide was out, but the waves were gently lapping the shoreline. Adults and children were running in and out of the water trying to keep cool. The sun was low enough in the west, that the patio was almost entirely in the shade.

The waiter stopped at their table and Fred ordered two beers. He told the young man that they would have something to eat later and to please leave the menus. Waiting for their beverages, the two turned their chairs away from the table and leaned back. Putting their feet up on the railing in front of them, they watched the sunbathers run in and out of the waves.

"Now this I can handle. Closing my eyes, I feel like I don't have a care in the world," Brenda said, taking the icy brew from the waiter's hand. "Is this where you spend your Saturday afternoons, detective?"

"Sometimes, but I must say it's especially enjoyable with you here to share it with me."

Brenda slowly sat upright, seemed to withdraw from the conversation. *Damn,* he thought, *I lost her. Be careful, Fred, you dumb ass. Take your time with her.*

"Brenda, where did you just go?" he asked softly.

"What do you mean, where did I go? I'm right here."

"I said something you didn't like, or that bothered you. Can you tell me about it?"

"Fred, I like my work. I want to do a good job. There isn't room for anything else. I thought you wanted to be a friend, but then you make some remark that sounds like something more than friendship. I told you, I don't date."

"But there has to be some reason why you think a *date* is so terrible."

"Okay, you asked for it. I was almost the victim of a date rape. It happened just before graduation at CMU. I'd been seeing this grad senior. He seemed nice enough, but then one night he slipped something into my drink. Then...if it hadn't been for my roommate barging in, looking for me, I..." Brenda stopped. She took a deep breath. "There! Now, can we just enjoy our beer?"

"It's okay, Brenda, you don't have to go on. But I'm not that guy. I'm a simple fellow, who likes your company and wants to get to know you better."

"There's nothing simple about you, Fred Watson."

Chapter 22

— • • • —

"HI, BRENDA. I'll meet you in the lobby. Will your car be ready when we get to the service center?" Catherine asked, cradling the phone under her chin, as she turned off her computer for the day, grabbing a portfolio of designs she wanted to work on at home.

"Yup, the little cruiser is greased, filtered and ready to roll for another three thousand miles. I'll be up in the lobby in a jiff," Brenda said, turning off the lights in her lab. She stepped out into the hall, and then checked to be sure the door was locked.

The two women met in front of the elevators, exited through the lobby door, and climbed into Catherine's stifling hot car. Catherine turned the key in the ignition and immediately put the AC on full blast.

"I'm telling you, Cat, if this heat doesn't let up soon I'm heading back home to Juneau."

"Only a few more weeks and the temperature will break. I've always found August to be the hottest month of the year." Catherine pulled her silver BMW out of the company parking lot and merged into the afternoon traffic.

"I hope you don't mind stopping at the House of Beads. I told Tillie and Pete I'd check in on the progress of the cyber café." Catherine flipped on her left turn signal and headed north to Ormond Beach.

"Not at all. I'm anxious to see your project and meet the characters in your capitalist venture." Brenda chuckled. "Fill me in on the cyber café—how did you get involved?"

"It started quite tragically," Catherine said, repositioning the AC vent on her side to blow directly on her face. "Russell's wife, Julie, died suddenly while she and I were attending a bead class."

"What did she die of? She must have been quite young."

"Julie was only in her early thirties. She was given an overdose of a drug, murdered, by the hand of Russell's arch competitor, Douglas Bradshaw. Anyway, I became friends with the shop's owner, Tillie Brown. She called me a few months back to get my thoughts on the space that had opened up adjacent to her shop. Tillie thought she might expand, but if she did she really had to add a different business, but something compatible with her current shop—more beads would not support the space."

Brenda adjusted the AC on her side and stuck her face in front of the vent.

"I know you'll like Tillie," Catherine said. "Then there's another character, Pete Peterson, otherwise known as Daytona Pete. He's a veteran and electronics whiz, but his passion is betting on the horses from his computer. I've been told he calls his living room his OTBP, off-track betting parlor."

"Okay, what's the connection between betting and beads except that they both start with a *B*?" Brenda asked.

Catherine laughed. "No connection and no betting. Pete is a very special person. He was Hutch's best friend." Catherine unconsciously put her hand on her belly—her lover's image filling her thoughts. Her breath came a little faster, as she tried to maintain her composure. "Excuse me, Brenda. It's still hard to even say his name." She put her hand back on the steering wheel and blinked several times to redistribute the teary water gathering in her eyes.

"Anyway, Manny, and Hutch for that matter, said they wished Pete would get out more. So I asked him to meet Tillie and me in the vacant space to see if he would be interested in consulting on the project—the cyber end. I told Tillie that if she liked the idea and the numbers added up, I would back the project. To make a long story short, she did, Pete did, and now the renovation is just about complete. Hopefully they will open for business in a month. You won't see any computers today, just the raw space painted and the floor tiled. I have to admit I want to get your impression of the idea and the space as a business."

— • • • —

Catherine pulled into the plaza and parked the car. "There's Pete's red Thunderbird parked in front of the shop. Your coming with me today is perfect. You'll get to meet both Tillie and Pete," she said, her excitement growing to see how the project was shaping up. "Just wait until you meet Pete. You'd never guess he's a double amputee the way he jets around in that T-bird."

"He sounds like quite a character," Brenda said, catching Catherine's excitement.

"Yes, Pete's all of that. He was in Iraq when he lost both legs below the knee, but he's no *sorry-for-myself* person. He's very humorous and generally has everybody around him laughing. He used to prefer a wheelchair. However, when he came over to the see the space the first time, he *walked* in. I thought Tillie was going to faint at the sight of him. He's very handsome."

"I can't wait to meet them," Brenda said, linking her arm through Catherine's.

"I think Pete may have taken a liking to Tillie, because I've only seen him walking since that day. He seems to have abandoned the wheelchair."

Catherine and Brenda entered the bead shop and were immediately hit with the strong odor of paint and then glue from the floor-tile cement. Tillie came rushing through the doorway from the adjoining space when she heard the jingle of the silver bell on the door.

"Oh, Catherine, I'm so glad you're here. Sorry about the smell. It got so bad I closed the shop this afternoon."

"Heavy odors seem to go along with progress, Tillie. I'd like you to meet Brenda Kittles. She's Stone & Associates' information technology VP."

"Nice to meet you, hon," Tillie said. "Please excuse the mess." The two women shook hands as Pete walked through the door from the café side.

"Well, well, what do we have here? One pretty lady has now turned into three. This is certainly my lucky day," Pete said, as he gave Catherine a peck on the cheek.

"Pete, you're as debonair as ever. I'd like you to meet Brenda Kittles. We work together, and I imagine the two of you have much in common—you both are besotted with computers," Catherine said laughing.

"Nice to meet you, Pete," Brenda said, extending her hand. "Sounds like you may have a tiger by the tail trying to keep up with the ideas these two women dream up."

"That is an understatement, Miss Kittles. However, I'm enjoying every minute of it, but don't tell them that. Follow me, ladies. The painters have just finished and are picking the canvas up off the floor—an unveiling of sorts." Pete turned and headed for the archway separating the bead shop from the cyber café. "Now, my darlings, watch your footing. I think the tiles are even, but I haven't tested them all with my trusty smart feet."

The parade entered the café with Pete in the lead. Tillie, her hand on Pete's shoulder, looked at Catherine to see her reaction. Catherine walked to the bay window in the front of the café, and then turned around to get the effect of the buttery yellow walls next to the large terracotta floor tiles. She looked up to check the medium blue ceiling, which cut down about a foot into the top of each wall. Brenda took in the space wide-eyed.

"Brenda, a mural painter will be here in a couple of days," Catherine explained, "after the paint dries completely." She dug out a Van Gogh landscape print from her portfolio case and held it to the wall. "The muralist will use this print as the idea for the walls depicting a French farm scene. The yellow walls are the canvas for the wheat fields, the stucco farmhouse, and out buildings, with red tile roofs. The blue ceiling is the backdrop of the sky, and she will paint fluffy clouds and a couple of birds in flight—pelicans and snowy egrets. The mural will encircle the tile floor and hopefully give the impression of a patio."

As Catherine described the mural, Brenda saw the space come to life. Pete took Tillie's hand as the two could feel the vibrant scene unfold.

Catherine again opened her case and pulled out six Van Gogh floral prints. "Tillie, here are the prints I suggested we put in shadow box frames. Please give them to Jo when she comes, so she can incorporate them into the mural."

"How do you envision using the prints?" Brenda asked.

"I thought Tillie could match the dominate color in each print with strands of her beads, tying the products of the two shops together," Catherine replied.

"Cat, I'm blown away. Promise me you'll bring me over again when the mural is finished," Brenda said.

"Hey, wait until you see my piece of the action," Pete said. "The furniture is scheduled to arrive in two weeks. Jo said she would be finished with the mural by then, at least far enough so we wouldn't be in each other's way. The computer salesman promised he could deliver the computers within two days of my call. Then darlin' Tillie here and I will set to work assembling everything."

"Is the computer company sending someone over to help you?" Catherine asked.

"Yup, but I think I'll only need him for a day—to do some of the positioning of the heavier pieces." Pete patted Tillie's hand as he spoke.

"Excuse me," Tillie said. "I opened a bottle of wine, so we could have a mini-celebration. I'll be right back." She scooted into the bead shop, returning with a tray holding a wine bottle and four plastic cups. "We have to work up to real glasses," she chuckled. "After all, this is just the beginning." She poured a little wine in each glass, handing the first two to Brenda and Pete. Picking up the third, she offered it to Catherine.

"Tillie, I'm afraid I have to pass this time. However, you've given me a perfect opportunity to let you and Pete in on my big news." She looked into Pete's eyes, and continued. "I'm going to have a baby. Pete, I'm going to have Hutch's baby." Catherine couldn't hold her emotions in check this time. Her eyes welled up and a tear slid down her cheek.

Pete came over, folding Catherine in his arms. Fishing in his pocket for his handkerchief, he dabbed her eyes as well as his own.

"Catherine, bless you. I'm so happy for you," he said, as he kissed her cheek. "Thank you for sharing this beautiful news with us."

Tillie stepped in and gave Catherine a hug. "When is this little bundle going to make an appearance?"

"Late January," Catherine replied, as she took the handkerchief Brenda offered her. "It's truly a miracle. Pete, I'm so glad you were here today, so I could tell you in person. I was going to call, but this is better."

Tillie again whisked back to the bead side and reappeared with a cup of ice water.

Pete raised his plastic cup to Catherine's, "Here's to Hutch's baby being brought into this world by the beautiful love of his life, Catherine."

Chapter 23

— • • • —

VICTORIA DRESSED QUICKLY. The stranger, who just called, said to meet him in thirty minutes at the Pink Pony bar. He told her to look for a bald guy wearing a black T-shirt with Harley Davidson written on the front. He would be sitting at the counter on the far left side.

His message was enticing. He told her that he knew of another big photo opportunity at the multiplex development site. She wasn't thrilled about meeting a strange man in a bar, but what the heck. The information sounded worth the risk. It had been four weeks since her group's last demonstration, and she was eager to organize another one.

Victoria climbed into her eleven-year-old, gray Ford Escort wagon and headed south. Pulling onto the narrow asphalt strip the small bar provided for parking, she was surprised there weren't more cars. It was eight o'clock on a Wednesday night, and she thought the place would be hopping.

She entered the bar and looked to her left. Sure enough there was a bald guy at the end. Two other patrons, a young woman and a man, sat together at a small table to her right. She slowly walked over to the man and sat down on the bar stool next to him. Neither spoke for what to her seemed like forever. Then he flagged the bartender.

"Bring the little lady a root beer, Mac."

"Sure will," the bartender said, with a grin.

"Excuse me. I didn't come here to have a drink, and if I did, it would certainly not be a root beer. Did you call me?" Victoria asked, turning to the man, looking him in the eye.

Mac returned with a glass of ice and can of root beer. He poured the soda to the midpoint of the glass. "There you are, little lady. Would you like some peanuts to go with that there *root beer*?"

"No thank you," she replied, her lips pursed into a thin line.

"Now that's not very hospitable, Victoria," the bald man said.

"You seem to know my name, so tell me yours. And what's this information you think you know, that I don't, about the building site?"

"Let's just say a little bird told me that Stone & Associates is going to lay the cornerstone for the first building, the hotel."

"So, what's so newsworthy about that? Of course, they would lay a cornerstone...sometime."

"You're a sassy one aren't you? Do you know when, miss high and mighty, because I do?"

"No, I don't know when. Why don't you tell me?" she asked, mimicking his derisive tone.

"It's scheduled for this Saturday at eight in the morning. They don't want any publicity. I guess they're afraid you and your cronies might show up."

"Why are you telling me this?"

"Let's just say I have a vested interest in the project, missy."

Chapter 24

—•••—

THE WHITE VAN, carrying Russell and his project team, turned down the access road to the beach and then continued south to the hotel building site. It had been over four weeks since they'd gathered for the groundbreaking. He asked Catherine and Brenda to bring their cameras. He wanted some still photos, and a couple of video clips he could send to the media outlets.

The beach was quiet except for a family scampering to collect a few shells as a wave receded. It was still hot and very humid for the middle of September, but there wasn't a cloud in the sky. Neither was there a breeze coming off the sparkling blue water.

"I guess no one told Mother Nature that the hot days of summer were supposed to subside by now," Russell said. "When we finish here, we'll head back so you all can enjoy the rest of your weekend."

The van drew up a few yards away from the site. A large rectangular granite block swung lazily from the end of a crane. Sanchez had directed the movement of the crane so it was positioned over the spot prepared for the cornerstone. Sanchez and a couple of his men, carrying yellow hard hats for the team, walked over to the van. As the vehicle disgorged its occupants, each was handed a hat and then fell into line behind Russell. Brenda and Catherine spread out in a wing formation behind their colleagues and started snapping pictures.

The team neared the site where the cornerstone block

was to be placed. Sanchez scooted over to Catherine. "Here, let me have that camera for a minute. You and Brenda get over by the others so we have some pictures with the two of you as well."

"Thanks, Chuck. It's all set," Catherine said. "Just press the button." She handed him the camera and joined Brenda with the others.

After Chuck took several shots, Catherine retrieved the camera and she and Brenda fanned out once again.

"Okay, Chuck, lets—" Russell was interrupted mid-sentence with the noise of two choppers approaching overhead. More noise came from the north, mixing with the chopper blades. Driving onto the beach was the big green bus with its horn honking, cutting into the sound of the gentle lapping of the ocean's waves.

"Damn, how did they find out?" Russell growled. "Come on, Chuck, set that block down. It seems we're going to have spectators whether we like it or not."

"Right, sir."

Chuck motioned to the crane operator. Six of his men circled the block as it was slowly lowered. Inches before it hit the ground, the men nudged the great stone to the place it would rest for years to come. Chuck waved both of his hands, palms down, signaling the stone was aligned. The block was lowered, gentle as a whisper, inside the orange painted outline.

The News 13 and Channel 9 choppers flew in formation slowly over the group but not before the protestors started shouting. They waved their signs, and several yelled once again into bullhorns. "We pay taxes. We want access."

Russell dialed Manny's cell number to ask for help in clearing the demonstrators. Unfortunately, it was too late. The news choppers already had the ugly side of the story. Exactly what Russell had hoped would not happen. With the cornerstone in place, he led his team back to the van. Chuck caught up with him just before Russell climbed in to take a seat.

"I'm sorry, Russell. I don't know how they found out. Someone had to have tipped off the news channels. Only the crane operator knew of our plans, so he could get the crane and the granite block into position. I didn't even tell the crew why I wanted them to come in this morning. I see that Victoria person is out in front of everyone again. Anyway, I'll see what I can find out."

"Thanks, Chuck. See you Monday morning for our team meeting. When the officers get here, tell them what happened, but I doubt they can do anything. The demonstrators were on the public beach, stayed clear of the site, and they didn't block any roads."

Russell looked back at the protestors and locked eyes with Victoria. "She's one smart cookie—made lots of commotion for the media, but savvy enough not to break any laws," he mumbled. "I wonder what her real beef is?"

Chapter 25

— • • • —

CATHERINE WAS RUNNING a little behind schedule for Russell's weekly team meeting. She hurried up to her home studio and turned on her PC. It was late last night when she finished working, so she'd downloaded the file to the server at Stone & Associates before going to bed. Having saved the file, her plan was to print the document in the morning. She wanted to show Russell's staff a couple of new ideas, plus some changes to the conference center.

"Miss Catherine, I brought you a glass of milk and a muffin," Lucy said, putting a breakfast tray on the coffee table in the client's corner of the room. "You were scurrying around so fast this morning, you didn't stop to eat. You have to keep up your strength you know."

"Lucy, you're an angel. Thank you." Catherine took a sip of milk and a bite of muffin as she sat in front of her monitor. "Whoa, that was quite a kick, little one." *I'm just as anxious for you to make an appearance, as you are,* she thought. Now well into her fifth month of pregnancy, her tummy was beginning to bulge, and the baby was becoming very active.

Holding the glass of milk in her left hand, she took another sip as she started to manipulate the mouse to pull up last night's design file. After several attempts, she set the glass down and leaned back in the chair. "That's odd," she said. "I could have sworn I filed it in the conference center folder." She made several additional attempts to find the file but came up with nothing to show for her efforts.

"Well, Catherine," she said, "you'll be late if you don't get going." She gave her computer the shut-down command. *I'll ask Brenda to find the file for me when I get to work,* she thought, *but right now, my dear, you'd better be on your way.*

— • • • —

Catherine parked her BMW in the company's lot and walked briskly to the side door, and then remembered it was locked. Scurrying around to the front entrance, she made her way down to the computer lab. She pressed the buzzer, and a second later the latch clicked to allow her to enter. Ben had installed a second button on the wall near Brenda's desk, so she could trigger the lock to release without having to walk over to the door. Brenda was sitting in front of her monitor with a large printout beside her. It was obvious she was comparing the printed page to whatever she was viewing on the screen.

"Cat, hi. What's up?" Brenda asked.

"Oh dear, you look like you're deep in thought. I hate to bother you, but I can't find a CAD file I saved last night. I was wondering if you could find it for me. I must have been blurry eyed and filed it in the wrong folder."

"Did you download the file to the company server?" Brenda asked.

"Yes. It was about nine o'clock and the name is confer-rev5. Russell is starting his weekly design review in fifteen minutes, and I wanted to show the team my latest ideas."

"Let me take a quick look," Brenda said. A few minutes later, Brenda looked up at Catherine and asked, "Did you save it on your home system before you downloaded it to the mainframe here at the company?"

"Yes, I followed the instructions you gave me. I always save the last edits at home and then download them. I probably worked another hour, maybe until ten or ten-thirty and downloaded my changes again. You're not telling me you can't find it are you? Look, I have a printout from two days ago showing the filename."

"I am telling you the file does not exist, in any iteration, on the system," Brenda said. "Cat, I'm not sure what happened to the file, but let me check the system logs from seven o'clock last night. Did you shut your computer off last night?"

"Oh, yes. I always do, but...come to think of it, I guess I didn't last night. The system was on this morning. I never gave it a thought. I was so intent on listing the changes I wanted to present to the group this morning."

"Well, it's unlikely, but possible mind you, that an intruder accessed your computer through the network. They would still have to know your user ID and password for your home computer, but if the computer was running—"

"I always turn it off. Last night was an exception. Exceptions will bite us every time, won't they," Catherine said, closing her eyes, shaking her head.

"Can you call Russell and let him know you'll be a few minutes late to the meeting?" Brenda asked. "Also let him know you and I would like to see him now, before the meeting."

Catherine relayed Brenda's request to Maggie, who said she'd pass it on to Russell. He was on the phone at the moment. Ten minutes later the two women entered Russell's outer office and found him standing at Maggie's desk.

"I don't like the looks on your faces," he said, as they followed him into his office. "What's up?"

"Cat's latest design, which she updated last night from home, is missing. Russell, it's been five weeks since the intruder visited our system." Brenda said. "I thought I had succeeded in shutting him out. But, now it appears a design file has been deleted. I need some time to go over the events of the last twelve hours. I'll also check with our leased-line company to see if they can come up with an explanation."

"Do whatever you have to do, Brenda," Russell said.

"I have one request," Brenda said. "Let's keep the disappearance of the CAD file between the three of us and, of course, Manny's team. I don't like this, Russell. I don't like it one bit.

Someone has definitely gained access to our passwords, or an insider has decided to perpetrate more than a prank. Maybe both."

— ••• —

Catherine and Russell left for the conference room and his design review meeting. Brenda returned to the computer lab to start her search for the weasel that penetrated the computer system. But first, she sent a system-wide email message to all the users requesting they change their passwords before leaving for the day. She added a PS at the end: "This request is part of a routine security requirement."

Taking out her journal, Brenda made the entry of the sequence of events as Catherine had related them to her. She then put in a call to the technician responsible for S&A's leased line—the firm's backup service, and ISP connection to the internet. She gave the tech the name of the file, and the date and approximate time it was saved and closed. He said he would check and call her back.

Making entries into her logbook of the steps she was taking, she proceeded to check the system log file between the hours of eight and eleven o'clock the night before. Nothing was amiss, but more important, at 9:03 p.m. Catherine's file was listed, but at 1:02 a.m. it was gone. No keystrokes were captured showing somebody had been there other than Catherine. All tracks of an intruder were brushed away.

The leased-line tech returned her call, reporting nothing appeared unusual from his end. He had Catherine's missing file on their backup storage disk. The file was copied on the routine backup at midnight. Brenda asked him to restore it to her server. She then purchased and downloaded a program she could use to trace and identify an IP address and its location. Her plan was to trigger an automatic print command of all keystrokes when someone accessed the system from an unknown IP address. "He might wipe away his footprints from the system, but they'll be captured on the printer," she mused, as she turned to her logbook entering the purchase of the software, and how she planned to begin implementing it.

"I don't know who, or where you are, but I'm going to find you," she said, clicking the program's install button. Once the download was complete, she began the task of setting up the parameters on how she wanted the program to operate.

— • • • —

It was almost midnight when Brenda returned home to her room in Catherine's house. Lucy had left a couple of cookies out on the counter with a note stating that there was a plate with chicken parmesan in the refrigerator. If she wanted a glass of chardonnay, the bottle was open alongside the chicken.

"Bless you, Lucy." Brenda zapped the chicken dish in the microwave, poured a generous glass of wine, and headed into her bedroom. She changed into her shorty nightgown, splashed cold water on her face, climbed into bed.

Sitting back against the headboard, she picked at the chicken, and slowly sipped her wine, pondering the day's events. A soft rap on the door signaled a visitor. Climbing out of bed she opened the door to find Catherine.

"Brenda, do you want to chat for a few minutes or would you rather turn in?" Catherine asked, holding a glass of milk.

"Actually, I'm glad to see you," Brenda replied, holding the door wide for Catherine.

The two women climbed on Brenda's bed and sat facing each other, but Catherine was the one leaning back against the headboard.

"Brenda, thanks for retrieving my file today. You saved me a lot of work. Well, actually weeks and weeks of work. I received your message asking everyone to change their passwords. Russell told me that Tom Balfor also changed all the project passwords. How could anybody from the outside get in?"

"There are very limited options to gain access to the network and server—logging into a user's personal computer with their password, access to the project space—again with a password, or logging into the System Manager account, otherwise known as a super-user. Then there are the employee offices. Ben changed all the codes on the office doors that are equipped with keypads. We're tight as a drum. I also changed the system manager's user ID and password again, and I opened a second email account for myself. You, Russell, and I are the only three with the highest level of security access."

"Brenda, do you think someone from the inside is responsible for the weird things that are happening to the system?"

"Well, it's either someone from the inside, or someone from the inside is giving their passwords out inadvertently, or on purpose, to one or more people on the outside. It would have to be a very savvy user, a person with programming abilities, to know what to do if they managed to get into the system manager account. I'm most concerned about the company's intellectual property—your department's schematics and design specifications that go with them. Plus there are the millions of dollars being deposited at the bank to fund the operation."

Brenda was now sure she had a full-scale hack job on her hands. But who is it? That was the question.

Chapter 26

— • • • —

IT WAS 7:30 IN THE MORNING and Parisians were beginning to hustle to work. Le Café de Cyber de Cappuccino had one customer sitting at station number three. A gentleman dressed in business attire, his suit jacket slung over his right shoulder, entered the café. A twenty-something clerk looked up from a fashion magazine, acknowledging the entrance of the new comer.

The sign on the counter, in French as well as English, welcomed the stranger and listed the price of renting a computer by the hour. Looking over his shoulder, the man could see into the computer room. The only customer, sitting with her back to the entrance, her monitor visible from where the man stood, looked to be playing a game. She had a cup of coffee beside her monitor and was clicking frantically trying to move the figure before it was swallowed by what appeared to be a gorilla-type monster.

"Peux-je vous aider, monsieur?" the young girl asked.

"English please, Maria?" Her name tag was pinned to the collar of her white short-sleeved blouse.

"Of course, sir. Do you wish to buy some computer time?"

"Yes, probably an hour."

"Please sign in, sir, while I start your computer. I will also need to see some identification."

The man signed the log, including his address and telephone number. He pulled out his driver's license and handed it to Maria, who had returned from starting the computer at station number five.

"Merci, Mr. Richards. Just let me make a copy of your license, and then I'll give you the password to log on to the computer."

"Merci, Maria. I would also like an espresso with whipped cream and a dash of nutmeg on top."

The girl made a copy of the driver's license. She then returned the license, as well as a password written on a slip of paper, to the man. Mr. Richards went over to the computer, set his briefcase on the table, loosened his tie, and sat down. With the slip of paper in front of him, he typed in the password. The café's internet home page immediately displayed. Station five was in a perfect location for his purposes. He was in the corner, back to the wall, facing the young woman playing the game and the door to the computer room. He could see anyone walking up to the counter. No one could sneak up behind him. Maria brought him his cup of espresso with whipped cream and nutmeg.

"Can I help you with anything else, Mr. Richards?"

"Merci, Maria, I'm all set," he said, looking up at her with a smile on his face.

Maria went back behind the counter, and again turned her attention to the fashion magazine.

Mr. Richards rummaged around in his briefcase, pulling out a small notepad. His fingers flew over the keyboard. Every now and again he referred to the information written in his little book.

"Yes. That will do it," he whispered to himself. "Stupid woman. Try to find me!" Taking a sip of his coffee, he turned the page on his notepad, and again attacked the keyboard. He worked slower now, verifying every keystroke to be sure he was reading his notes correctly. It was now 8:10 in the morning in Paris, which meant it was 2:10 a.m. on the east coast of the States. Twenty minutes later, he leaned back in his chair with a barely audible sigh, followed by a quiet chuckle.

Once again he sat forward attacking the keyboard. He turned back to the first page of the notepad, and, referring to the information, seemed to get the results he wanted. "That one is for you, Mr. Stone," he said to himself. He quickly logged off the machine, deposited the notepad into his briefcase, and snapped it shut. He put on his jacket and walked to the counter to pay for the time he used the computer.

Maria took the money and counted out his change.

"Keep the change, Maria," he said with a smile.

"Merci, Mr. Richards."

Mr. Richards stepped out the door of the café and melted into the stream of early morning business workers. He dropped an envelope containing Mr. Richard's driver's license and the café's receipt into a sidewalk trash receptacle as he strolled by.

Passing another small café full of patrons buying their morning coffee to take to work, he paused, looked around, and then went inside. He edged his way through the crowd to the tiny men's room in the back. It was unoccupied. He entered and locked the door. *Luck is with me today,* he thought. He pulled off his reddish-brown wig stuffing it in the waste container by the sink. "Bye bye, Mr. Richards," he said to the image in the mirror.

Exiting the lavatory, he moved into the crowded café. Edging his way to the front door, he stepped out into the morning sun shining brightly over Paris—the next to last day of September.

Chapter 27

— • • • —

THREE WEEKS HAD PASSED since Catherine's file was destroyed. "Figures, I get ready to catch the rat and he goes back to his rat's nest," Brenda mumbled, as she pulled out of Catherine's driveway, heading to work. The sun hadn't been up long—she wanted to get a jump on the day. On the way, she stopped at Krispy Kreme for some high-test coffee and a doughnut. The cashier suggested a baker's dozen was a good buy. Brenda didn't take her up on the offer. A zap of sugar from one doughnut was all she needed.

Arriving at her desk in the lab, the first thing she did, with coffee and doughnut at hand, was to scan her journal for all the procedures she had performed the day before. Throughout her computer forensic courses, and the jobs where she had to track down hackers, the one thing her professors and bosses demanded was *document everything you do*. Sometimes it's the only record that will stand up in a trial.

She turned to the monitor and logged into her new corporate email account—a new account that only a few people knew about. She was trying to whittle down potential suspects from inside who might be responsible for the unexplained events. She was startled to see a full-screen message, similar to the one she had received almost a month ago as a desktop graphic, but this was definitely an email, triggered, on opening her email account, to display full screen.

"Hello, Brenda. Did you miss me?

Time for your next lesson. In chess, the Pawn usually moves first. There are eight of the poor little devils, all lined up to take the brunt of the onslaught. The big guys hide behind them. Rather like you, Brenda. You are a pawn waiting for my attack. Sorry, but I'm afraid you will have a rather unpleasant day. Goodbye."

This time the background was jet black and the words a bilious yellow. Some of the characters looked as if droplets of blood were falling from them—an embedded graphic in the message. The sender identification, in the header of the email, was blank. *Damn,* she thought, *he used one of those anonymous service providers.* She knew such services were offered to people who didn't want to be identified. The provider rented out an account for a daily, weekly, or monthly fee. The person buying the service could configure an email anyway he wanted, such as leaving the sender blank. She closed the message and logged out of her email account as well as her user account.

She sat staring at the monitor, her mind racing for an answer as to how the message pierced all her efforts to block ChessMan. *So much for going home at night,* she thought, as she opened her journal to a fresh page: "Sept. 29, Monday, 7:13 a.m. Opened an email from an unidentified sender."

The question is, she thought, how did he know my new email address?

With a fresh cup of coffee in hand, Brenda again began the tedious job of scanning the system log file. She found three email log entries from an employee to recipients outside the company: Jack Fatigate at 6:30 p.m., Tom Balfor at 6:42 p.m., and Ben Sitwell at 7:00 p.m. At 10:00 p.m. Brenda found a log entry into the system by Balfor. Ben Sitwell sent a message out at 10:40 p.m. The anonymous message to her arrived on the server at 2:29 a.m. Brenda noted these events, including time, in her journal.

Fatigate, Balfor, or Sitwell could have sent her new email address to ChessMan, or did he get into the system and read the email address file through some hole in the operating system she wasn't aware of? She retrieved the emails the men had sent—nothing seemed unusual. All were addressed to a known recipient, no blanks. Which still begged the question: did someone gain access to the system email file containing the usernames, IDs, and passwords?

Brenda initialized the tracing software. She found the route of the message she had received. It came through an ISP address, which she soon determined was in Paris. The Paris leased-line host showed it was assigned to a cyber café, and listed the café's name and telephone exchange. Because of the time differential, she was able to reach the café on the telephone.

A woman answered. "Bonjour, le café de cyber de cappuccino."

"Hello, do you speak English?" Brenda asked.

"Yes."

"I'm calling from Florida, U.S.A. I'm looking for someone who sent me a message from your café. The time stamp shows the email was sent at 8:29 this morning, your time. Are you open at that hour?"

"Yes. We are open, what you say in the states, 24-7?" she said, with a little laugh.

"How many were using the computers at your café at that time? Do you know?"

"Well, I guess it is okay to give you that information. Let me check the sign-in sheet. Ah, yes. There were two—a man and a woman."

"Can you give me their names, please?"

"*Oh, no.* I cannot do that."

"I understand. You've been very helpful. Merci. Goodbye."

Brenda hung up the phone and immediately dialed Fred's number at the department. "Let's see, it's after nine o'clock. He must be in by now or out chasing some criminal."

"Hi, Fred, it's Brenda."

"Well, are you calling to invite me to dinner, so you can pay the whole bill this time?"

"Very funny. I'm calling to update you on ChessMan. Can you come over? I'm in the lab."

"Sure. How about I pick up some fresh coffee? Of course, I expect you to reimburse me," he said chuckling.

"You can be so annoying. You know that don't you? Yes, a large coffee, two creamers, would be appreciated."

"No sugar? Oh, wait a minute, you don't want to be too sweet."

"You got that right. Now stop with the chitchat and get your brown body over here."

"Yes, ma'am."

Brenda disconnected the call. "That man can be so exasperating. I should have called Manny," she said, as she pitched her empty cup into the wastebasket.

Brenda immediately picked up the phone and called Russell.

Hi, Russell, can you come down to the lab for a minute? I have some stuff I want to show you."

"I was just about to call you, Brenda. I received a strange email this morning, but I can't tell who sent it."

"What did the message say?"

"Here, let me read it to you," Russell said, calling the message up on his screen.

> *"Your computer guru is playing a game of chess,*
> *I suggest you check her next move,*
> *To make sure she doesn't create a mess."*

"Come on down and I'll show you my message, plus what I'm doing to try to cleanup *his mess*," Brenda said.

Chapter 28

— • • • —

RUSSELL PUNCHED in the keypad code, and he and Catherine entered the lab. Brenda gave them a brief update showing them her message, and Russell handed her a printout of his email. Catherine read them both, and looked up at Russell.

"Brenda, where do we start? Who do we notify?" Russell asked, as he paced around the lab. "Do we keep all these events quiet, or tell the staff? Call Homeland Security? What?"

"Russell, do you recall the message I received as a desktop graphic a month ago referencing a game of chess? What we received today was definitely a step up from that. ChessMan is taunting us."

"Yes, I remember. He talked about a game of chess."

"That's right, but not playing a game. He was explaining the rules of the game. I have already traced my email back to its origin in Paris. I will trace yours as well, but I bet they came from the same place."

"Paris is certainly a twist in the scheme of things isn't it," Catherine said, again scanning Brenda's email.

"Yes, it is," Brenda replied. "I called Detective Watson, and he's on his way over here. After I fill him in on what I found so far, I'll ask him if he could use his contacts in Paris to get the client's name and description from the cyber café."

"Good. Let me know what he finds out. What do you suggest we do about notifying our employees of a potential problem?" Russell asked.

"Well, we could warn users through emails that their activities may be monitored and remind them once again of the necessity to practice good computer security."

"But that would alert someone on the inside that we're on to suspicious activity," Catherine said.

"Unfortunately, that's true," Brenda replied. "Another way of thinking, and personally the way I would like to proceed, is to keep this to ourselves until we actually know what happened. The more we talk the greater the risk of an insider sweeping his or her tracks under the rug, so to speak."

"Okay, Brenda, let me know if Fred succeeds in obtaining any information from Paris," Russell said, his face lined with worry. "The murder, the demonstrators, the explosion, and now these computer breaches—it feels as if Stone & Associates is being hacked to pieces in front of my eyes."

Chapter 29

—•••—

FRED ARRIVED with the prescribed large coffee. Juggling two coffees, a small sack with stirrers and creamers, and a briefcase with some information from Dani, he still managed to punch the buzzer to the right of the lab's door. An immediate click answered the buzzer. He pushed the door open with his hip, but one coffee landed on the floor. Brenda looked up at the sound of the coffee hitting the tile and jumped up to help.

"It's okay, Brenda. I didn't need any more coffee anyway. Here's yours."

"Fred, I'm sorry. Here, I'll split mine with you," she said, retrieving the empty cup she'd tossed out earlier.

"That will be four bucks, miss," Fred said, wiping off his shoes with a napkin.

"Hey, come on. What do you mean four bucks?" Brenda said, pouring half of the hot coffee from one cup to the other.

"Geez, you really are a piece of work. So, give. What did ChessMan do that caused you to lure me over here?"

"Are you working on the other investigation, the murder, or are you not?" Brenda asked, with a decided edge to her voice.

"Truce, Kittles. Tell me what's got you so riled up."

"First, let me show you the message I received this morning." Brenda logged into her new email account and showed Fred the message. "Please note the sender is not identified. That space is blank."

"Did you know how to lineup the pawns?" Fred asked with a smirk.

"Come on, Fred, pay attention. Yes, I have played chess, and yes, I know where the pawns lineup to start a game. Here's a copy of the email Russell received. The timestamps on the two messages are just minutes apart—mine was sent first, then Russell's."

"Okay, what do you want me to do?"

"I traced the message back to a cyber café in Paris. It was—"

"Wait just a minute, how did you do that?" Fred asked.

"With my trace-route software program. It showed me the ISP location, the name it was registered to, and the contact number. Think of it this way," Brenda said. Picking up a pen and a piece of paper, she started to draw a diagram.

"When you mail a paper envelope, it travels from one post office to another, to another, etcetera, until it gets to your post office, which delivers it to you at your home or business. A postmark is stamped on the envelope at its place of origin—where you mailed it." Brenda took a sip of coffee, and turned the paper over ready to draw another picture.

"An email travels the same way except it's from hub to hub on the internet. It travels along the superhighway, the internet, to your email inbox. However, the email is coded with the address from where it was sent—the internet service provider of origin's ISP address."

"Now, that is some cool detective work."

"Yes and no. As a rule, a cyber café won't give out the names of its customers—privacy considerations. In short, while I could determine from which computer the email was sent, the staff at that location would not tell me the name of the customer who sent it."

"I see. Now, you want me to pull some strings and get the name and description of the sender," Fred said, leaning back in his chair, drinking the last drops of his coffee.

"Bingo! I've done practically everything for you," Brenda said, handing him a sheet of paper. "Here's the name of the café, its address and telephone number, and a copy of the email with the header information. I'm also giving you a copy of my journal entries today. Do you think you can find out who this guy is?" Brenda asked, looking intently into Fred's eyes. All signs of her earlier sarcasm were replaced with quiet desperation.

"Brenda, I think there's a good chance I'll have some information for you before the day is out. We have reciprocal relationships with police departments in most major cities around the world." He wanted to give her a hug but decided not to risk it...not yet anyway.

— ••• —

After Fred left, armed with her investigative procedure logs, and the cyber café information, Brenda called the Florida Computer Crime Center. She was told politely, but with a chuckle, to call back if she had evidence of an actual crime and not some prankster playing a chess game. The same story came from Homeland Security—understaffed and overworked with long lists of what they considered *real* crimes. "Call your local law enforcement department," the voice said, and hung up.

Chapter 30

— • • • —

DANI AND GEORGE entered the bullpen, both laughing over an incident on Law & Order. "It so would *never* happen that way," Dani said. "Sometimes that show gives us such a black eye."

"I agree," George said.

As they rounded the corner they could see their boss had that look in his eyes. His ramrod straight body, coupled with his hurried writing on the board, told them they'd better knock off the joking.

"Morning, Manny," they both said in unison. Peaches was the only one who looked up. Manny didn't seem to hear them, engrossed in adding to his theory list. Sensing George and Dani were at their desks, he asked, "Where's Fred?"

"Right here," Fred said, entering the bullpen.

"Glad to see you could join us, Detective Watson." Manny pushed the save button on the third board, cleaned it, and then turned to face his team.

Fred sat down and took a long drink of coffee. I had a meeting with Brenda—"

"Ah, even more time with the beautiful computer lady," Dani said, raising her eyebrows.

"Yes, the very *professional* computer lady, Miss Trotter," Fred retorted. "She called me this morning requesting me to come over to see the latest emails. It seems both she and Stone had a message deposited in their inbox early this morning with the *sender* left blank. She had already traced the messages when I arrived. She found that they came from an ISP in Paris. Until this Paris event, she and I had started to formulate a hypothesis for an inside job."

When Fred said *she and I,* Dani and George's eyebrows shot up again.

Ignoring their antics, Fred continued, "Catherine Hainsworth's deleted CAD file could have been an inside job."

"What if it's an outside job?" George asked. "In which case, the theory that the cleaning man was murdered for his keys to the building, and made to look like robbery, is plausible? That would mean the hacker was able to get enough information to hack, but then Kittles kept tightening the screws on the security. Is the lease-line company aware of the computer breaches?"

"Not the whole story. They're responding to Brenda's security requests, and they were successful in restoring Catherine's missing CAD file," Fred said. "The messages are becoming more ominous. The whole thing seems like a vendetta, but by whom and why?"

Manny went to the board and added computer hacking to the list, also added the words: "Nexus to murdered man?"

"George, do you have anything more on the protestors?" Manny asked.

"No. But as Fred was talking," George said, "let's not forget Victoria Standish has a doctorate in computer programming. The company she works for specializes in installing, programming, and troubleshooting networks for their clients."

"This is good," Manny said. "At least we're coming up with some credible theories. Under the presumption that the hacker is an insider, who would you add to the suspect list?"

"I've been thinking about that," Fred said. "Sitwell and Fredricks have been with the company for several years. Fatigate, Balfor, Sanchez, and Kittles are all new to the company. I can't imagine Kittles is involved. She's really stressed out and called for help when she found the message this morning. I've already contacted our counterpart in Paris to see if he can get the name of the café's client, hopefully even a description."

"George," Manny said, "do some digging on Balfor and Sanchez, as well as Victoria Standish. Fred, go ahead and work on the Paris angle, and do some more digging into the backgrounds of Sitwell, Fatigate and Fredricks. We can't assume anything."

—•••—

"Hi, Brenda. I have good news and bad news. Which do you want first?" Fred asked, holding the phone to his ear with his shoulder as he tapped his pen on a sheet of notes he had just written down.

"Give me the good news first," Brenda replied. "I could use some."

"An officer in Paris went to the cyber café. The clerk checked her files and did find a driver's license for the person who was using the computer yesterday. The one that matched the ID you traced. In fact, she was on duty and remembered him. It seems he gave her a rather nice tip. Anyway, his name is Henry Richards. It was a Georgia state license. She also had his address and phone number from the customer logbook."

"That's wonderful. What else?"

"What else is the bad news. Nothing checked out—bogus license, address, and phone number."

"Any kind of a description?" Brenda asked.

"Hey, now you sound like a cop. Sadly, not much. The woman thought he wore a suit, average height, average brown hair, but he was very nice."

"Great," Brenda replied in an irritated voice, "just your average chess player."

Chapter 31

— • • • —

"IS THIS MS. KITTLES, Ms. Brenda Kittles?" Fred asked in a mock-serious tone.

"Why, yes it is. And to whom am I speaking?" Brenda said keeping up her side of the banter.

"This is Detective Watson. I'm in Stone & Associates parking lot, under the shade of a Queen Palm tree. I've come to rescue you, my pretty damsel, from your dark, mushroom infested dungeon."

"Umm. I see. It so happens I'm not exactly dressed appropriately—no white flowing gown, no glass slippers—"

"Exactly what are you wearing," Fred interrupted, "in that cold, musty place you call a laboratory?"

"A pair of jeans, white T-shirt and white sneakers—no fancy slippers."

"Perfect," Fred said. "I'm sure you haven't noticed, but it's lunchtime, so come on out and play, Kittles. I'm going to whisk you away for an hour of fun and culture."

"Culture, huh? I'll be out in a jiff."

— • • • —

With a smile on her face, Brenda logged out of her email, slung her small bag over her shoulder, and locked her lab door behind her. She ran up the stairs to the first floor, and quickly stepped through the lobby. Scanning the visitor's parking lot for Fred, her eyes landed square on his grinning face. Revving the engine of his Harley a couple of times, he rode up beside her.

"Here's a helmet," he said, tossing a shiny black globe to her. "Hop on the seat in back of me."

"Fred, you've got to be kidding. I haven't ridden a motorcycle since my dad took me for a ride when I was ten."

"As they say, you never forget how to ride a bike, and one with a motor is even easier."

"Okay," Brenda said, strapping on the helmet. She swung her leg over the seat and wrapped her arms around Fred. "I think you did this on purpose, detective, so I'd have to cling to you."

"Hey, what a thing to say," he said, again feigning seriously being hurt by her words. "Hang on my fair one. We're off to the cultural event of the season."

—●●●—

Fred maneuvered the big black Harley through traffic, being mindful of the rules of the road. He was enjoying the closeness of Brenda holding onto him for dear life.

From the moment they left the parking lot, Brenda heard the increasing noise of motorcycles, lots of motorcycles. Before they'd ridden far, they were surrounded by bikers. On Route 1 they passed open-sided tents, which seemed to have sprung up over night. Brenda could see they offered all kinds of T-shirts, helmets, and leather gear for sale. The stalls were packed with customers. They'd parked their bikes so close together you couldn't walk between them. Music blared, balloons fluttered in abundance, and hot-dog carts all added to a carnival-like atmosphere.

When they neared the causeway, bike traffic was so thick only an occasional car was seen. The cars that did manage to squeeze in were encased with bikes. Fred drove up over the U.S. 92 causeway to the beach side of the city. Stopping at the red light before turning onto Peninsula, Brenda yelled into Fred's ear over the din of the motorcycle noise, "What's happening? Where did they all come from?"

"This, my beauty, is known as Biketoberfest," Fred yelled back. "They come from all over the U.S. and many from Europe and Asia. It's a huge event here that happens every year in mid-October."

The throng turned left in tandem onto Peninsula. It looked like a slow moving train, bikes all bunched together, but somehow not ramming into each other, or falling over. Most of the bikes were driven by men with a biker babe behind him. There were also bikes operated by females, hair drawn back into ponytails, or covered with a small bandana. Many men with beards, ponytails, and heavy black leather jackets rode noisy bikes of metallic purple, silver grey, and shiny red.

The dance of the bikes turned right onto Main Street. Many peeled off immediately, as did Fred, into the Boot Hill Saloon parking lot. It was jammed full of bikes, and hot rock music poured out of the cement-block bar.

"Fred this is crazy," Brenda said laughing happily, taking it all in.

"You ain't seen nothin' yet, my lady. Let me have your helmet and we'll lock up."

— • • • —

Fred took Brenda's hand and led her into the bar. It was thick with bikers. A group of four guys stood on a platform playing electric guitars and singing full tilt. A long bar was straight ahead with a row of booths alongside. The balance of the space was standing-room only.

They made their way to the shiny bar and scooted down to the end to a vacant stool near the front door. Fred patted the seat indicating that Brenda should take it, and that he would stand alongside her. A cute young girl, short black hair, silver hoop earrings, wearing a tank-top with Boot Hill Saloon strategically silk-screened on the front, asked for their order. Her upper arms sported several tattoos.

Fred leaned in over the bar so she could hear him. "Two beers and a couple of turkey clubs, please. Is that okay with you?" Fred asked, talking directly into Brenda's ear.

Brenda looked up, smiling, nodding in the affirmative.

The walls were plastered, floor to ceiling with license plates. Pictures of bikers and their babes were interspersed here and there. The bar top, and booth tables were laminated with saloon posters of glamorous girls, as well as bikers of all ages, and bikes of all makes and models.

The bar girl set their icy-cold beer bottles down on the shiny surface—no glasses in this wild saloon.

"Wow, Fred, look." Brenda nodded her head indicating that Fred should look up over his head. Above the bar hung a row, tightly spaced, of ladies bras in a multitude of cup sizes. "Fred, check out the lacy black number. That woman would have to have serious back issues."

Their sandwiches arrived and they dug in. The music was not conducive to conversation. Fred pointed to a poster which read, "You're better here than across the street."

Brenda turned to Fred, a quizzical look on her face.

"Cemetery," Fred said, nodding his head in the direction of the other side of the street.

Brenda nodded, that she got it, as she swayed back and forth on the bar stool, moving to the beat of the music.

They finished their sandwiches and Fred fished out his wallet. He paid the bar girl and indicated that she should keep the change. Brenda took one last look around as she slid off the barstool. Startled, she grasped Fred's arm as he was turning to leave.

"Fred, look. In the booth at the far end."

Fred followed Brenda's gaze. His eyebrows barely moved as he saw what she was looking at.

"Fred, it's Jack Fatigate and Victoria Standish," she whispered her lips touching his ear. "What would those two, of all people, be doing together?"

"Good question," Fred said, as he and Brenda slipped out the front door.

— • • • —

Fred bounded up the stairs to the bullpen. Dani was busy in her lab and Manny and George were away from their desks. On a clean corner of the whiteboard, Fred wrote: "Saw Fatigate and Standish in a bar, heads together." He added his name and then drew a squiggly line around his note. Satisfied, he headed back to Brenda and his motorcycle.

Chapter 32

— • • • —

THE TRAIN HURTLED at over two-hundred miles per hour through the yellow fields of Paris and up into the green slopes of the Swiss Alps. The passenger, weary from having spent several weeks in Europe house hunting, leaned back in his seat enjoying the view of the countryside whizzing by. Reaching its next stop, he could feel the train begin to slow its forward motion as it approached the Bern station in Switzerland.

The TGV train came to a halt after much screeching of wheels as they gripped the rails. The passenger from Paris picked up his bag and disembarked the car. Walking briskly down the steep hill, he headed for the UBS AG, where he had an appointment with one of the bank's officers. After filling out several forms, he gave the bank official a cashier's check in the amount of $134,000—the minimum required to open a Premier account available to United States' citizens.

His business accomplished, the man stopped at a nearby café. He ordered apple juice and a fresh salad, which came layered with ham. The man knew it would be several hours before he enjoyed another meal, so he ate slowly enjoying the rustic café complete with wooden beams. The other patrons seemed to be businessmen taking a break in their busy schedule, on this mild, sixty-eight degree day in mid-October.

He paid the waitress for his meal and left the café. A slow smile crossed the man's face when he noticed a computer store on the opposite side of the street—a boutique he surmised because it was so small. He changed his course and crossed the street. Entering the shop, he looked around and saw a computer in the corner on a high stand. A sign above it said, "Try it, you'll like it." The shop was empty. After all, it was lunchtime—time to eat, not to buy a computer.

"May I try your computer over there?" the man asked.

"Certainly, sir. Can I help you, perhaps explain some of the features?" the young shopkeeper asked.

"No, that won't be necessary. Is it connected to the internet?"

"Oh, yes."

"Well, that's nice. I'll give it a spin."

The man stood in front of the screen, his back to the shopkeeper. He opened the computer's browser to access the internet. Pulling a notebook out of his breast pocket, he thumbed to the page he was looking for and carefully began to strike the keys. The man put the notebook back in his pocket, and briskly continued typing. Finished, he closed the browser.

"Thank you," he said to the young man minding the store. "It is a fine machine. However, today, I'm just looking."

The two nodded to each other and the man left. It was 3:08 p.m. in Bern; 9:08 a.m. in Daytona Beach.

The man retraced his steps up the steep hill to the train station. He purchased a ticket on the next train to Zurich, scheduled to leave in thirty-five minutes. He browsed through the main terminal floor and stepped behind a very high display case. No one was in his line of sight, so he grabbed his baseball cap, pulling it off his head along with wispy brown hair attached to the cap. The man quickly stuffed the disguise into his suitcase's side pocket and walked out of the terminal building to the waiting train. He boarded his car, put his suitcase in the overhead bin, and settled back in his seat for the hour trip. *Mission accomplished,* he thought, smiling as he closed his eyes.

Chapter 33

—•••—

BRENDA HELPED CATHERINE up onto the examining table. Catherine had asked her if she would mind coming with her for the ultrasound appointment. It was scheduled for the first slot in the morning, and then they could go on to work.

Laying back on the cold surface, she lowered her head to the small pillow. The room was painted a pale yellow—a neutral color, not pink or blue. Soft piano music filled the room from a speaker in the corner. The temperature was a bit chilly. The johnny gown Catherine was asked to put on barely covered her and gave no warmth.

"Brenda, thanks for coming with me. I'm excited and a little nervous at the same time," Catherine said pulling the cloth of the gown tighter over her growing belly.

Brenda stood beside her friend holding her hand, softly rubbing her fingers to warm them. "Are you kidding? I was thrilled when you asked me. I wouldn't have missed this moment for anything. Cat, do you really think we'll find out the sex of the baby?"

"That's what I'm told. This should be my twentieth week and Dr. Colton said there is a very good possibility he can tell. At first, I wasn't sure if I wanted to find out, but the more I thought about it, the more I wanted to know. I decided I would feel even closer to this little person if I knew."

The door to the examining room opened and the ultrasound technician came in. She was dressed in a brilliant white topcoat, a contrast to the short black curls swirling around her head. She carried a chart, her mouth bowed into a pleasant smile.

"Hi, Mrs. Hainsworth. My name is Betty. How are you feeling today?" she asked, as she pulled the equipment with the monitor a little closer to the examining table.

"I'm just fine, thank you. A little nervous I guess, and please call me Catherine. I'd like you to meet my friend, Brenda Kittles."

"Hello, Brenda. I'm glad you're here to share this moment with Catherine. There's a chance we won't be able to tell for certain if it's a boy or a girl. A lot depends on the position of the baby. A little guy may not be ready to show himself," Betty said with a little laugh.

Catherine immediately liked Betty. She knew there was a chance they might discover an abnormality but had immediately put the thought out of her mind. Her pregnancy had proceeded without a problem, so there was no reason to be apprehensive— nervous was acceptable, however.

Betty draped a sheet up under Catherine's stomach then opened the gown and laid the fabric to her sides leaving only her belly exposed. "Ultrasound provides fantastic high-quality images. It's completely painless, and simple, and doesn't involve radiation like an x-ray," Betty said. "I'm going to spread a conducting gel on your belly. It will feel a little cold at first, but warms to your body temperature quickly."

As Betty began spreading the gel, she told Catherine what she could expect.

"When the gel is in place I'll move a wand-like instrument across it. The wand emits high frequency sound waves which penetrate through the gel and your skin. As the sound waves penetrate various body parts, they are relayed to the ultrasound machine which constructs the images you will see."

"Well, my techie friend," Catherine said looking up at Brenda, "how does that sound to you?"

"It's fascinating, Cat. Tell me if I squeeze your hand too hard, but I'm not letting go of you," Brenda said.

"How long will this take, Betty," Catherine asked turning her head to look at the technician. She could also see the monitor, but at the moment the screen appeared like a television that had lost its signal, all snowy.

"Oh, I imagine you'll be up and dressed in less than an hour. Here we go."

The static-filled screen slowly began to show fuzzy areas in different shades of gray. Betty very slowly moved the wand over Catherine's belly from side to side and sweeping around.

"Catherine, there's your baby. My, my, aren't we the active little one. I think he wants to kick the wand, like it's a football teed up for a field goal."

Betty's eyes were trained on the monitor as her hand continued to slowly move the wand. Catherine and Brenda stared mesmerized at the developing images. Brenda raised Catherine's arm, holding her knuckles under her own chin. She didn't realize her eyes were watery.

"Betty, you just said *he* was kicking the wand like a football," Catherine said. "Are you telling me something?" Catherine's pulse quickened, every fiber of her being straining to see the moving image on the screen.

"Yes, Catherine, unless I'm mistaken, you're going to have a baby boy. What do you think of that?"

Catherine turned her head from the monitor and looked up at Brenda. Their tearful eyes locked. It was written on Brenda's face that she understood how wonderful this news was to her friend. Tears welled up, spilled over their lashes, trickling freely from the eyes of both women.

"Well, I guess from your reaction that you're happy. Your doctor has to confirm my findings, but I think he'll agree. Would you like me to print a picture for you?"

"Oh, yes. Please." Catherine said, still clutching Brenda's hand.

Betty turned off the machine and began to wipe the gel off of Catherine's belly. "There you are, my dear," she said, helping Catherine sit up on the edge of the table. "Let me get the picture from the printer next door. I'll be right back."

Betty immediately returned with the printed picture of Catherine's baby and handed it to the expectant mother.

"Look, Brenda. The baby is definitely a little guy," Catherine said. Brenda had her arm around Catherine, holding her close as the two friends looked intently at the image.

"Thank you, Betty," Catherine said. "When will I hear something from Dr. Colton? Will he also tell me if everything looks normal?"

"He should be back to you with the results in a few days, and, yes, he can tell if the baby appears healthy. But I don't think you have anything to worry about. You can get dressed now. I hope you enjoy your day," Betty said, helping Catherine off the table.

Catherine gave the woman a hug. "You'll never know how happy you've made me. Thank you, Betty."

As Betty closed the door to the examining room, Brenda wrapped her arms around Catherine. Catherine went limp in Brenda's embrace, lowering her face into the crook of Brenda's neck. "Brenda," she whispered through her tears, "I can't believe this miracle. Hutch must be smiling down on me. He has to be happy he's going to be a father, and of a football player to boot."

Chapter 34

—•••—

BRENDA TAPPED in the code to her lab door, entered, flicking on the overhead lights. Thoughts of Catherine's baby, and the miracle she had seen were still with her. It was now almost eleven o'clock, and she certainly needed the Starbucks coffee she treated herself to get her mind in gear.

Settling into the desk chair, she logged into her email—anonymous had sent her another message. This time there were no clever graphics—the characters in Arial, 10 point, dated today.

> *"Hello, Brenda.*
>
> *I only have a minute—we're always in a rush aren't we. I did want to get back to you with the moves of two more of the chess pieces, the knight and the bishop. They really are minor pieces, and not deemed nearly as valuable, or powerful, for that matter, as the rooks or the queen. Of course, like people, not all are as worthy as you and I. Wouldn't you agree?*
>
> *The knight jumps in an "L" formation, in any direction he likes. This nimble Rumpelstiltskin can jump over and around other pieces. Clever fellow, he is the only one that can pop over others. Ah, but if he lands on you, dear Brenda, then he captures you. The bishop is very staid and only moves diagonally but in any direction. If he is positioned on a black square at the start of the game, he must remain on the black square. No wiggle room for this stately fellow. If you are in his path, he snags you as well.*

I'm afraid I have to run. Until next time..."

Brenda immediately fired up her trace-route software. The email had originated in Bern, Switzerland, at 3:08 p.m. TraceRoute displayed the ISP address, the name of the business, and a telephone number.

"It's a little after eleven in the morning here. With any luck, someone may still be at work—plus six hours, makes it five o'clock there." Brenda decided to give it a try, and dialed the number. It didn't go through. She forgot about the country code. After getting all the routing codes, she dialed again.

"Bern Computer Supplies, may I help you?"

"Yes, hello, I'm calling from Florida in the States. My name is Brenda Kittles. Whom am I speaking to?"

"Hans Reich, miss."

"Mr. Reich, I do have a question, and I wonder if you might help me?"

"I'll try, but I may have to attend to a customer."

"No problem. I received an email this morning. Actually, it was sent at 3:08 this afternoon, from a computer located in your shop. I'm trying to locate this person because I need more information. Do you sell computer time?"

"No, we don't. But we do have a display model that is connected to the internet, so customers can try the machine."

"Do you keep a record if someone uses that computer?"

"No. The machine is merely for a potential buyer. If they like it, we build a computer with the same specifications."

"I see," Brenda said. "Were you by any chance in the shop at 3 o'clock?"

"No. I was out of town. My son was minding the store for me."

"Oh, do you think I could speak with him?"

"I'm sorry, miss, he's on a train to London, returning to school."

"Okay, well, when you speak with him, will you ask him if he remembers someone coming into the shop, about three, and if so, could he give you a description. I'll give you my telephone number, just in case he remembers something."

"I'll be glad to, but when I asked him about the day, he said there were only a couple of, what you call in the States, tire kickers," the man said, laughing.

Oh, that's just great, Brenda thought. She gave the man her name again, and telephone number.

"Thank you for your time, Mr. Reich."

"No problem, miss. Have a nice day."

"You, too, Mr. Reich. Goodbye."

"Another dead end," she said, reading the message again.

Chapter 35

—•••—

"HELLO, MRS. HUTCHINSON? Meredith Hutchinson?" Catherine asked, her voice hesitant, her heart beating against her chest.

"Yes, this is Meredith Hutchinson."

"Mrs. Hutchinson, we've never met, but I knew your son, Stephen—"

Catherine heard the woman on the other end of the line take a quick breath. "Mrs. Hutchinson, are you still there?"

"Yes. Who are you?"

"My name is Catherine Hainsworth—"

"Catherine?" the woman whispered.

"Yes. Stephen and I—"

"My dear Catherine?" the woman said softly. "Yes, I know who you are. My son called me a few days before...before he was killed. He told me he had met a woman. He said her name was Catherine. He said...he loved her." Mrs. Hutchinson could hardly speak. "I wanted to try to find you, but I didn't know if I should...and now, now you have reached out to me."

"Mrs. Hutchinson—" Catherine began to say, tears welling in her eyes at the news that Hutch had told his mother about her.

"Please, Catherine dear, call me Meri."

"Meri, I would very much like to come to Newburyport to meet you. I don't want to intrude, and, if you'd rather I didn't, I'll understand."

"Oh, my dear, please, please come. Come as soon as you can."

—•••—

"Lucy. Lucy, are you in the kitchen," Catherine called out.

"Yes, Miss Catherine. Is something wrong? Are you all right?" Lucy asked hustling into the hallway, as Catherine carefully descended the stairs.

"Yes, everything is fine. Everything is wonderful. Lucy, I'm going to ask you a very big favor."

"Anything. Heavens, Miss Catherine, tell me what has you so excited."

"Lucy, I just talked with Meredith Hutchinson."

"I don't understand."

"Mrs. Meredith Hutchinson, Hutch's mother. Lucy, she was so nice. She spoke with a slight British accent, and, Lucy, she wants to meet me as soon as I can get there."

"Miss Catherine, where does she live?"

"Newburyport, in Massachusetts."

"I've been there," Lucy replied, wiping her hands on her apron.

"I've already called Dr. Colton. He gave me the go ahead, but said to be careful and not to overdo. He did say that if I'm going to travel to do it soon. I really don't want to travel alone. What do you think? Lucy, could you come with me?"

"Oh, my. This is happening so fast. Of course, I'll come with you. How far is Newburyport from Portsmouth, New Hampshire?"

"I don't think it's very far. I drove that way once going to Maine for a vacation with my parents. Why?"

"I have an aunt in Portsmouth. I haven't visited her in years. I could see you safely to Newburyport and then go on up to Portsmouth. When do you think you might make the trip?" Lucy asked.

"This coming weekend."

"Oh, so quick?"

"Yes. Meri, her name is Meredith but she asked me to call her Meri, said to come as soon as I can, and that even this weekend would be perfect. Lucy, call your aunt. I'm going to check on flights. We certainly want a non-stop, and I'll rent a car—"

Lucy couldn't catch her last words as Catherine went into the library to start making their reservations.

— ● ● ● —

Lucy drove the rental car out of Boston, then on to Route 95 north. An hour later, using Catherine's Google map, she exited off the highway into the quaint city of Newburyport.

"Lucy, I'm a bit nervous. Meri was so warm and friendly on the phone, but I didn't tell her about the baby."

"Miss Catherine, she's going to love you, and to think you're carrying her grandchild—"

"I know. I know. It's going to be overwhelming. Let's see, the directions say we turn left here, two more blocks, and then right." Catherine looked up from the map. There it is, Lucy. Meri said it was an old, 1850, red-brick townhouse. Look, Lucy, there's even a picket fence. How New England is that?"

Lucy parked in front of the house. Catherine got out of the car, straightened her blue wool skirt and white blouse, which covered most of her tummy. It was fairly obvious she was pregnant, after all she was now in her seventh month. She walked slowly up to the front door, with Lucy following close behind. Catherine was about to lift the brass doorknocker when the door opened.

The two women, one with soft, silver-gray hair framing her face, slight of build, and the other a striking blonde, gazed a moment into each other's eyes. Meri took in the sight of the woman standing before her, then seeing Catherine's protruding belly, gathered her into her arms. She knew this woman was carrying her son's baby.

Neither could speak. Tears flowed freely, as Meri led Catherine into the cozy townhouse, complete with fireplace, beamed ceiling, and wide, pine floorboards. Lucy followed shutting the door quietly behind her.

"Oh, excuse me, Meri. Where are my manners?" Catherine said, moping away the tears. "I want you to meet Lucy, Lucy Sullivan. She kindly came with me—I didn't want to risk traveling alone.

"Lucy, welcome," Meri said, as she too dabbed at her eyes with her handkerchief. "I have plenty of room, so I want you to make yourself at home."

"Thank you, Mrs. Hutchinson, but I'm driving on to Portsmouth to visit my aunt. I'll be back the day after tomorrow to pick up Miss Catherine. But thank you anyway. I best be on my way—you two have a lot to talk about. I know I'm leaving her in good hands."

Catherine went over to Lucy, gave her a hug and a whisper of "thank you" in her ear.

— • • • —

The following two days were bitter sweet for both women. Meri had already brought out several old photo albums of Hutch as a baby, then as a toddler, and growing up on into grade school. Then, not so many when he left home to attend boarding schools in Europe. His parents felt it important that he learn many languages never dreaming he would use this knowledge as an undercover agent. She had pictures of him returning home for Christmas holidays, and some from his graduation at the University of Michigan. There his story seemed to end.

"On his last trip home before graduation," Meri said wistfully, "he told his father and me he was going into government work, a special section. He asked us not to worry about him, but, of course, we did. Unfortunately, we didn't see him much after that. What a treat it was when all of a sudden he would appear on our doorstep. He'd stay a few days, and then leave, disappear really."

"Oh. Oh my, that was a healthy kick. Here feel," Catherine took Meri's hand, laying it on her belly.

A smile crossed Meri's face as her eyes lit up.

Catherine explained, "I think little Stephen is going to be a football player."

"Stephen?"

"Yes. I had an ultrasound a few days ago, actually the day I called you. When I found out the baby was a boy, I knew his name would be Stephen. Are you pleased, Meri?"

"Oh,…yes…Stephen." Meri gently put her hand back on Catherine's swollen tummy. "Stephen."

Chapter 36

— • • • —

STONE'S BODY LANGUAGE said it all—he was bone-tired and depressed. "Good morning, Maggie. Anything new I should be aware of?" he asked with a sigh.

Maggie followed him into his office. "Are you okay, Russell? You don't seem yourself this mornin'."

"I'm fine, just a little tired. Thank you for asking."

"I'll get you a nice cup of coffee then. That'll perk you up."

"Yes, thank you," Russell said absently. He walked to the window of his office, looking out on the street below. The murder, the demonstrations at the construction site, and the computer events were weighing on him. However, deep down he knew the real reason for his malaise was the fact his wife was no longer with him. At first, following her sudden death, he thought he could cope with his loss. But as time went on his sorrow and loneliness deepened. Everyone told him it would take time to heal, but instead of healing, the wound festered. He didn't care about the project anymore. The daily issues that kept arising were the only things that kept him focused.

"Here's your coffee, Russell. It's pipin' hot."

"Thanks, Maggie. Close the door on your way out, if you would please. I have several reports I need to deal with, and I don't want to be disturbed."

"Russell, Catherine called and wondered if she could pop in to see you. Do you want me to ask her to wait awhile?"

"No, no. Tell her to come on in when she gets here."

Russell turned on his PC, stepped back to the window while the computer started up. He heard a soft knock on his office door and then Catherine entered.

"Good morning, Russell. It's a beautiful morning, crystal clear and the temperature has dropped some. Sanchez should make good progress today." Maggie had alerted her that Russell seemed rather down today.

"Yes, I suppose so."

"Okay, Russell, give. What's the matter? You look like your best friend just died. Oh, that was a stupid thing to say. I'm sorry, but you do seem withdrawn. Is there anything I can help you with?"

"It wasn't a stupid thing to say, Catherine. My best friend did die. By the calendar it was months ago, but it seems like yesterday. I'm sure you know what I mean."

In a faltering voice, Catherine said. "Russell, they would want us to live our lives as best we can. It's up to us to fill the void ... somehow."

"I know, Catherine. It's strange isn't it? The one thing I wanted for Julie and me was to make this company a big success. I wanted to give her everything. It turned out that because of my work I lost her. I drove her into the arms of another man, Douglas Bradshaw," he said with such bitterness, he thought he might vomit. "Catherine, I'm not sure I can see the tower project through to its conclusion. I'm not saying I'm ready to hand it over to you as yet. I will certainly stick it out until you are on your feet again, but the reigns may be in your hands soon after that."

"Russell, you know I'll be there when you need me. But, right now, Mr. Stone, you must dig in your heels, throw those big shoulders back, and get on with your work," Catherine said smiling. "We've had enough of a downward spiral for one day."

"You're right and thank you." Russell turned, straightened his posture, and walked to his desk. He took a sip of coffee and logged into to his corporate email account as Catherine handed him an updated design for the reconstruction of the rundown pier, a part of the project.

"Catherine, look at this email from Victoria Standish. It's vile."

Catherine glanced at the message from over Russell's shoulder. Her eyes grew larger as she read.

> *"Subject: Checkmate*
> *Mr. Stone, this is to inform you that if you don't stop your loathsome construction on our beautiful, pristine beach, I and my followers will stop you. Do you hear me? We will bring you down!*
> *This is not a game, Mr. Stone. You are a wretched human being, who is only looking to enrich himself by destroying a piece of the planet that we mere pawns wish to enjoy.*
> *If you do not cease this despicable endeavor, we will cease construction for you.*
> *Very sincerely,*
> *Victoria Standish"*

"Russell, you should call Manny. Victoria has definitely crossed the line. She's threatening you with bodily harm, as well as the workers at the site."

"My thought exactly, but there's something else that's unsettling. Look at the words Victoria used. They echo some of those in the emails Brenda and I have received concerning a game of chess. Do you think she could be involved in our computer breaches?"

Chapter 37

— • • • —

"HI, BRENDA, I'm running a few minutes late," Catherine said. "Lucy is going to meet us in the lobby in ten minutes. We'll take my car. Is that okay with you?"

"Sure. You sound a little breathless. Is everything alright?"

"Yes, it is. It just seems like everything is happening at once. I'm so happy you and Lucy are going to the Lamaze class with me. The instructor said my request to attend was a few weeks early, but, when I explained your hectic schedule, she said to come along. I'll pick up the classes again when it's closer to my time."

Catherine cleared her desk. She had one more call to make before meeting Lucy and Brenda.

"Hi, Maggie, can you let Russell know I'm headed to a birthing class and will be back later...I know. It is exciting. Bye."

Taking one last look around her office, Catherine picked up her purse and rode the elevator down to the lobby. Lucy and Brenda were waiting for her and the three women headed out on a mission to learn about the event that was going to change their household forever.

— • • • —

"Good afternoon," the instructor said with a pleasant smile, looking around the room. "This is a happy occasion, because you can finally see you're coming up on the big day, the birth of your baby. We're first going to watch a short film on the birthing process, a little of what you can expect when you start your labor, through the time you welcome your baby into this world. Then we're going to take a little tour before we learn how to breathe—the kind of breathing that will help you relax. This is the time when your partner will help you the most."

The instructor started the film, and everyone immediately became engrossed in what they were seeing on the screen. Most of the mothers-to-be held the hand of the person who had accompanied them, Catherine included—Brenda on one side and Lucy on the other. When the film was completed, the instructor led the way to the maternity ward, where they had the opportunity to see the private birthing rooms. Then the big treat—the nursery.

Both Lucy and Brenda took out a hanky, Lucy handing an extra one to Catherine. Most of the women were seen dabbing their eyes, looking at the line-up of the precious bundles.

"Look how beautiful, and tiny, they are," Lucy said, her nose almost touching the window.

"They are wonderful aren't they," Catherine said, feeling that somehow Hutch was witnessing the little miracles behind the window with her.

Chapter 38

— • • • —

THE MAN'S EYES CLOSED. The slight sway of the train, and the rhythmic clicking of the wheels on the tracks, lulled him into a light sleep. The train entered a tunnel and the sound vibrations caused the man to wake, jerking his head up. Realizing the train was in the darkness of a tunnel, he let his chin drop, and his eyelids fell shut again. The screeching of brakes, and the change in momentum, caused the man to wake again, this time from a deep sleep. Startled, he looked around. Checked his watch. The time had flown by. The conductor came through the car calling out, "Zurich. Zurich. Exit through the back of the car."

The man stood and pulled his suitcase down from the overhead rack. He fumbled a bit, striking a young boy with his elbow as he set the case on the floor of the car.

"Excuse me, young man," he said, giving a slight nod of his head to the boy. The boy shrugged his shoulders, indicating he didn't understand.

He moved in line with the other passengers to the back door of the car. The man stepped down two stairs, and then turned to lower his bag to the platform. Heading to the terminal with his suitcase in tow, he followed the signs to the men's restroom. His eyebrows rose slightly when he saw there was an enclosed stall with a sign picturing a wheelchair. The man entered the stall, closing the door behind him. He could hear the chatter of two men at the urinals, then the splashing of water, then receding footsteps as they left the restroom.

The man put his suitcase on the toilet, pulled the zipper and opened the bag. He switched his trousers, pulling on a pair of baggy brown slacks. Even though the temperature was mild outside, he slipped a large sweater over his head, knitted out of brown tweedy yarn. He then fished out a shaggy gray wig, pulling it tight over his scalp. The gray hair wisped down over the neck of his sweater. He had not shaved for three days, so his overall appearance was that of a rather old man, who didn't care how he looked. The man carefully folded the clothes he had changed out of and placed them in the suitcase. Before closing the case he retrieved a telescoping wooden cane, slightly scratched. Listening to be sure no one else was in the restroom, he exited the handicap stall with his suitcase and limped out the door, steadying himself with his cane. Out on the street in front of the train terminal, the man limped to the cab stand. A cab driver quickly came to the man's assistance. The man asked the driver if he spoke English.

"Yes," the driver said. "Where would you like me to take you?"

"The Park Inn at the airport, please."

"Right away, sir. Let me put that case of yours in the trunk, and we'll be on our way."

Weaving in and out of traffic, the cab swung into the curved driveway of the five-story inn and let the man out. The driver retrieved the suitcase, and the man paid him the fare, with a less than generous tip. The man turned to enter the inn, but paused when he heard a plane overhead. Looking up, he saw the noise came from a jet airliner gaining altitude. The man entered the hotel and checked in at the reception counter.

"Thank you, Mr. Samuels. Would you like some help to your room?"

"That won't be necessary, young man."

"I hope you enjoy your stay," the clerk said, handing the man his room key.

Mr. Samuels took the room key and grasped the handle of his suitcase. With the aid of his cane, he limped to the nearby elevator. He punched the number three button and rode the elevator alone to the third floor. Stepping out of the elevator, he walked to his right down a hall to his room.

Samuels entered his room, closing the door behind him. He threw his cane on the couch, pulled off the wig and sweater, and laid the suitcase on the bed. His laptop was in the top outside compartment. He pulled the laptop out, set it on the desk, attached the internet cable to the wall's outlet, and then turned on his computer. Within a few seconds he was connected to the internet. Turning away from his computer, he picked up the telephone.

In a gravelly voice he said, "Hello. I'd like a 4:30 wake-up call tomorrow morning. How often does your shuttle leave for the airport? ...continuously? Thank you."

Samuels hung up the phone and turned back to his computer. He fished the small notepad from his pocket. Using the information in the pad, he entered the email account and typed in his message.

"Good evening, Mr. Stone. Or, maybe it is good morning depending on when you read this. It really doesn't matter when you read your email. You and Miss Kittles are pawns in my hands.

I'm sure Miss Kittles has shared my last message with you containing the rules for the knight and the bishop. To be honest, I'm finding the instructions quite tedious, but here goes. We shall now look at the rook and the queen. The rook is considered stronger than the knight and the bishop, although I'm not sure why. It moves in a straight line until it is blocked. If you are in my rook's way, it will capture you. Ah, but then there is the queen—the most powerful of all the pieces. You must watch out for her, because she can move in any direction, and go as far as she wants.

So now, Mr. Stone, we have but one piece remaining, the king. The stakes are moving higher. You will know what I mean in a little while.

Until then..."

Samuels saved the message. His plan was to send it when he got up in the morning so it would be waiting for Stone when he arrived at work. Satisfied, Samuels logged off the email account. Next he headed for the bathroom and a long hot shower. Refreshed, he returned to his room. Fishing out a small folder from his suitcase, he removed an airline ticket. Seeing the customer service number, he dialed the phone.

"Yes, I'd like to confirm my flight tomorrow morning on Spanair, leaving Zurich at 7:05 a.m. to Madrid, and continuing on with Aeromexico to Cancun. The name is Thompson...yes, I'll hold. Yes, yes, I'm here. I'm confirmed? Do you also have my flight to Miami, Florida, the following day? ...good. Thank you. Goodbye."

"Ah, time to order dinner from room service," he mumbled. After placing his order, he put his clothes in the closet along with his suitcase. Tomorrow would be another day of travel for the man with the cane.

Chapter 39

— • • • —

A SMALL CLUSTER of cars was parked in front of The House of Beads & Cyber Café. The Chamber of Commerce was holding a Business-After-Hours event to celebrate the grand opening of the new computer and internet service. Catherine had rented small round bistro tables to place in the big bay window of the make-believe patio in the café. There were also four more tables outside on the wide walkway for guests to gather.

Several bottles of red wine were waiting to be opened on a rectangular table inside the café. A tub of ice was on the floor discreetly to one side, keeping the white wine chilled. Several business owners from the area had already arrived and were genuinely surprised at the beautiful French scene depicted in the mural. Pete had installed speakers in both the café and the bead shop, and he diligently made sure the CD player continued to rotate with soft chamber music.

— • • • —

Brenda pulled into the plaza and parked. "This is as close as I can get," she said to Catherine. "Do you want me to drop you off at the front?"

"No, I can walk. It'll be good for me."

The two got out of the car and headed for the shop. "Catherine, this is so exciting—your first VC business is opening," Brenda said. "Can you believe it? I can't wait to see the mural."

"I'm excited, too," Catherine replied, "but especially for Tillie and Pete. They have put in many long hours getting the place ready for today. I hope there's a good turnout from the Chamber."

"How about that banner spanning both of the shops—Grand Opening" Brenda said. "It must be thirty-feet long. It looks like a fourth of July celebration with the streamers and balloons. I don't know what's sparkling, but it looks like beads floating under the words."

The two ladies entered the shop, but no tinkling bell today. Tillie had propped the door open to make it more inviting for her visitors.

"Catherine, welcome," Tillie said, greeting her benefactor with a quick hug. "What do you think of the banner?"

"Very nice. Looks like the event is beginning to build," Catherine said.

"Build, my love, you should have seen it earlier," Pete chimed in, planting a peck on Catherine's cheek. "We had quite a few students drop by after school. They had a grand old time playing games on the computers. Games that yours truly picked out—some new ones they hadn't seen before."

"Well, don't you look dapper, Mr. Peterson," Catherine said. "Let me look at you. You could be a French artist with your white painter's shirt and black trousers, but those black Italian loafers are something else."

"Glad you approve. Of course, the shoes pinch my feet," Pete said chuckling. "Hey, what do you think of my little darlin' Tillie, here?"

"I think you look like a matched pair," Catherine said smiling.

"I told her she has to wear this little black dress more often. It sends me into a swoon every time I look at her."

"Oh, go on," Tillie said, a red glow rising in her face. "Brenda, get in here. It's hard to squeeze a word in edgewise with these two. I'm so glad you could come to see the finished product."

"I wouldn't have missed it, Tillie," Brenda said smiling.

"Come. Follow me into my French cyber café." Tillie grasped Catherine's hand, leading her into the new space.

"Oh, Tillie, it is so much better than I had envisioned. Jo did a masterful effort with the mural. The shadow boxes with strands of your beads twinkling against the Van Gogh prints are striking. You did a wonderful job in selecting the colors."

"Can I buy a couple of the necklaces you're showcasing?" Brenda asked. "They're stunning," she said, moving from one shadow box to another. "Oh, I have to have this amber gemstone necklace."

"Oh, yes, dear, everything is for sale. If you look inside the box, underneath the print, there's a price tag for each piece."

"Where did Pete go?" Catherine asked. "I want to congratulate—"

"He's right here, my luv," Pete said, "with a glass of sparkling water for the little mother to be. You were saying—"

"Thank you, kind sir," Catherine said, accepting the glass from Pete and taking a sip of the fizzing water. "I was saying, I want to congratulate you on your layout of the kiosks with the computer stations."

"Do you like them? Saves space with just a flat screen monitor, keyboard and mouse. The monitors are connected to the computer in the back room. In fact, one computer is serving all the stations and the internet hookups for the laptops," Pete said, with pride. "Of course, there's a backup machine just in case the mother gets sick. You know how those pesky viruses float around."

"Hey, this is quite a place," Russell said, joining the group.

"Russell, I'm glad you could make it. I want you to meet Tillie. She's the owner of the bead shop and now the cyber café," Catherine said with a wink at Tillie.

"Mr. Stone, I'm so happy to finally meet you," Tillie said. She suddenly turned pensive as she looked into Russell's eyes.

"Tillie." Russell stepped forward and put his arms around the woman whose shop held the memories of his wife's last minutes before she died.

Russell slowly released her. "I wanted to come by before, but I just couldn't bring myself to do it. Today seemed like the right time."

Pete held out his handkerchief to Tillie, and she dabbed her eyes.

"Pete, my dear, will you do me the honor of pouring our guests a glass of wine?" Tillie said, with a soft smile. "Today is a day of celebration."

Chapter 40

— ••• —

BRENDA SAT STARING at her computer. Fred stood behind her reading another email with the sender field left blank. They were both mulling over who could be behind the emails. How much of a threat was the email from Standish, or was it just bluster?

Brenda had immediately set up a trace and found the current message had originated at the Airport Park Inn, Zurich, Switzerland. The registration desk then gave the standard reply, "We are not allowed to divulge the names of our guests." Too many hours had passed. The trail was cold.

"Fred, there's only one more chess piece, the king. The rules for the king will define the end of the game, *checkmate*." Brenda looked up at Fred, worry painted across her face.

"Brenda, it's almost eight o'clock," Fred said coming around to her side. You haven't eaten since breakfast I bet, and you're tired. Can I persuade you to come to my place so I can fix you dinner? We can brainstorm what's going on while we eat, and then I'll send you on your way home. What do you say?"

Brenda closed her eyes, with a small sigh. "You're right. I'm not going to accomplish anything more here tonight. Throw in a glass of wine, and I won't be able to turn you down."

— ••• —

Brenda followed Fred to his house. She was too numb to think about what she was doing. She didn't question that she was breaking her rule not to date, let alone go to a man's house for dinner. She pulled in behind his jeep and got out of her car. He walked her to his front door and let her inside, closing the door softly behind them. "Welcome to my humble dwelling. Come on, I'll show you around."

"First of all, detective, this is not a humble dwelling. This is a beautiful house, and do I see a pond in back, through the trees?"

"You do. It's manmade, and there's also a network of canals that handles the downpours, like you've seen in the past few weeks."

"Very impressive. I have to tell you, I've never experienced rain like you have here. But, as Catherine has said, they rarely last very long, and then the clouds clear out. She says she can almost set her watch by the storms. They seem to arrive every day between three and five in the afternoon."

Brenda walked into the living room. "Fred, the view is beautiful," she said, looking out through the screened porch to the water. "It must do wonders for your mental state to come home to such a tranquil scene."

"You've got that right," Fred said, walking back into the open kitchen area. He poured two glasses of Shiraz and then joined her. Handing her the goblet of red wine, she looked up into his eyes. For some reason, she didn't feel threatened from the warm look she saw there. In fact, she felt comfortable and more—she felt safe.

He tapped his glass to hers. "Here's to the first of many times when I hope you will do me the honor of coming to dinner."

She tapped his glass in reply, still looking into his eyes. *Yes,* she thought, *I hope there will be more.* The strain of the past few weeks seemed to float away.

"Brenda, if I kiss you, will you run away from me? Because if there's a chance of you fleeing I won't." Fred put his glass down on the coffee table. Brenda didn't flee. She didn't move a muscle. In fact, she couldn't breathe. She wanted to feel his lips on hers. He slowly put his hands on her shoulders, and then to each side of her face. He slowly put his lips to hers, very gently, then slowly pulled his head back, his eyes closed savoring her taste." He opened his eyes as she slowly opened hers. Neither spoke as he moved away, picked up his glass, and quietly went to the kitchen to prepare dinner.

— • • • —

Fred retrieved a large container of spaghetti and meatballs from the freezer, popping the lid slightly. He put the plastic bowl in the microwave and returned to her side. Adding a little more wine to each of their glasses, he sat down on the couch and patted the cushion, inviting her to sit next to him.

"Brenda, tell me what happened that night in college. I need to know so I can help us get to the other side of that experience."

She sat down, but turned away from him, looking out at the pond, staring but not seeing the water. "There was a party at one of my classmate's homes. His parents were away, but they said he could have a group over at the end of finals week. The bar was stocked, pizzas were delivered, and the music was playing. He and his friends rolled up the rug in the family room and everyone started to dance. I had accompanied my roommate to the party. She begged me to go with her. She said it would be fun, that we had worked hard, and we deserved a little downtime. I didn't have a car, but she did, so I went with her. I was having a good time, and I did know many of the kids."

"I take it, so far so good," Fred said.

"Yes, but then it changed. This guy I knew, from several of my classes, asked me to dance. Then we danced a few more times, and he offered me a drink. I told him I didn't drink much, but I would enjoy a glass of wine. He went to the bar, poured a glass of wine, and then suggested we go into the den, where the music wasn't so loud. We talked a little about one of the class finals we both had taken. Then suddenly I started to feel very tired, then weak. I told him I wasn't feeling well, that I felt faint."

"So this is when things started to turn ugly?" Fred asked.

"Yes. He said I'd better lie down, and he helped me out to the hall and then into a bedroom. I barely made it to the bed. That's the last thing I remember. My roommate told me later that she had seen me go with Steve to the den. It was getting late, and, when I didn't return, she went looking for me. She opened the bedroom door where I was and screamed. I mean, she said she really screamed. I was lying on the bed. My dress and underwear were on the floor, and Steve was naked, climbing on top of me. She said my wrists were tied with scarves to the bedposts."

Brenda stopped talking, her heart quickening as she relived the vision of that night.

"When my roommate screamed, Steve hurriedly put on his pants, as other kids, hearing the scream rushed into the bedroom. He evidently said he was just having a little fun, and wasn't really going to have sex with me. I was told he walked out of the house, slamming the front door as he left. My roommate untied my wrists, put my clothes back on me, and, with the help of a couple of other friends, got me into her car. I started coming around, but I was still very dizzy. The next morning, she explained what she saw when she entered the bedroom. I looked at my wrists. They were very red, almost raw. He had slipped one of those date-rape drugs into my wine." Brenda, rubbing her wrists, continued to stare out at the pond.

"Did you see him again on campus or in class?"

"No. We graduated a week later and I left school. Steve didn't go to graduation. In fact, he seemed to disappear. Nobody saw him after that night. My roommate thinks he ran, afraid I might press charges. I did see a doctor the next day, to be sure he hadn't raped me. The tests were negative. My roommate interrupted him before he could harm me. I still felt dirty and never told my parents what happened. Of course, the kids, who came into the room and saw me before my roommate could get me dressed, assumed the worst. I just wanted to get away, and put that terrible night behind me."

"You can trust me, Brenda," Fred said, taking her hand in his.

"You're the first person I've told. I want to bury the memory of what happened, but, of course, my mind won't let me. I've been on two dates since that time, in over five years. They were a disaster. I panicked each time and quickly left. When you and I met at the Aquarium for dinner—that was the first time I was able to control that panicky feeling. And then tonight, tonight...your kiss was so tender...so gentle. I wasn't afraid."

Chapter 41

— • • • —

BRENDA ENTERED the lab juggling a thermos of coffee, a bagel with cream cheese, and a banana in a zip-lock bag, as well as her briefcase. Lucy packed the little breakfast bag knowing how she frequently skipped this most important meal of the day. Setting her load on the table next to her computer, she pressed the Esc key to wake up her monitor. She was pleased to see the blue desktop come alive.

Thank goodness no messages today, she thought, unscrewing the thermos lid. The aroma of the fresh coffee brought a smile to her lips. Fred had insisted she have a cup of decaf before she left his home the night he had fixed her dinner. Her opinion of him had completely changed. In the days since he'd taken her to see his house, they'd met for dinner almost every night—a few times at a restaurant, twice with Catherine and Lucy, and a few times in the lab with take out when neither could spare time away from work. He was really very nice, she decided. He certainly treated her with respect, kindness and understanding. She enjoyed being with him immensely.

Yes, she thought, my life seems to be taking a new path, a very nice path.

"Good morning, Brenda."

Startled, the voice snapped her out of her dream world. She quickly looked around to see who had spoken. She didn't see anyone.

"Okay, where are you? This isn't funny," she said as she walked around the shelves holding backup storage drives, computer manuals, as well as the stacks of computer printouts of the system logs.

"Don't be afraid, Brenda. I'm not going to hurt you," the voice said.

"I'm not afraid of you. I can't even see you, so what's to be afraid of?"

"You're amazing. So smart. I know you tried to track me down, but I'm always several steps ahead of you. In a few days, I'll be able to show myself and offer you the world."

"I don't want the world," Brenda said, walking to the door of the lab. She snapped the light switch off plunging the lab into darkness except for the glow of her computer screen. "Who are you?"

"I can't tell you yet. I hope you're enjoying our little chess tutorials. The next piece is the king, and, of course, Checkmate. I have to go now, my love, but I'll be back. Do enjoy your day…somehow."

Brenda raced up the back stairwell to the third floor. She walked swiftly past Sally and into her office. She shut the door and leaned back against it, her heart pounding, fear pulsating through her temples. She heard her college roommate scream. She saw her raw wrists. The events of the awful night she was assaulted played out in her mind. Lifting the telephone receiver from its cradle, she fumbled in her desk drawer for Fred's card. Her hand shook as she punched in his cell number.

"Fred, it's Brenda. Something very strange just happened. Can you come over? I'll be in the lab."

—•••—

While Brenda waited for Fred, she walked around the lab and particularly in the direction where she thought the voice came from. She could see nothing. Then she scanned the ceiling for any kind of hole where a camera eye might be. Because of the shelving around her computer desk, the camera had to be confined to a very small area if it was trained on her chair. Then she spotted it, a black circle no bigger than a dime cut into the white ceiling tile.

The lab buzzer felt like a knife in her back. Looking over her shoulder, she saw Fred standing outside her door. Brenda picked up her journal, and her purse, and walked to the door. Flicking off the lights, she exited the lab, closing the door behind her.

"Don't say anything," she whispered. "Let's leave the building, and I'll tell you what happened."

"Okay, but Brenda what are you afraid of? Your eyes look as if you just saw a ghost," Fred said.

"In a way, I did. Can we sit in your car?"

"Sure, come on."

The two left the building, and for the entire world to see, they looked like they were going to a meeting. Once in the car, Brenda explained about the voice, which she surmised came from a man. A man saying he would be back soon to tell her about the king and checkmate. She knew he could hear her, and she also thought he could see her, because he knew when she walked around.

"Fred, I'm sure I located the camera in the ceiling over my desk, but I couldn't find the bug or speaker." Brenda looked to be in control of her emotions, but her hands were showing a slight quiver.

Fred took her hands in his and held them firmly. "Let me call Dani and ask her to meet us in your lab. If the camera is where you think it is, she'll be able to dismantle it without destroying any evidence. Once the camera is removed, we'll do a sweep to find the bug and the speaker."

"Ask her to meet us here in the parking lot. I don't want to go back in the lab in case he's still watching. That's why I picked up my purse as we left and turned off the lights. I wanted him to think I was leaving."

Fred called Dani and filled her in on what was going on, and asked her to bring whatever tools she thought she might need. He then called Manny and told him what happened to Brenda, and that Dani was on her way over.

—●●●—

Dani drove up shortly in an unmarked car and knocked on the window of Fred's jeep. "Hi, guys," Dani said with a smile, holding a cardboard tray with three large coffees.

"That coffee looks just like what the doctor ordered for my friend here," Fred said, opening the car door. Brenda slid out the other side.

"I have extra creamers and sugars," Dani said, handing a cup to Brenda.

"Thank you, Dani, this is perfect," Brenda said.

"Okay, everyone, let's get to work," Fred said, helping himself to the third cup and tossing the cardboard tray on the floor in the backseat.

When they entered the lab, Brenda pointed to the black spot in the ceiling where she thought the camera might be located. Fred spotted a step ladder next to the shelves and positioned it under the ceiling tile. Dani tore a piece of black tape from a roll in her kit and climbed up the ladder. She stuck the tape over the camera's eye and signaled Fred to hand her the box cutter she had laid on the table. Cutting around the tape, she quickly dismantled the camera from the ceiling. With a hand signal of thumbs up, and a big smile, she backed down the ladder. Brenda gave Dani a quick hug.

After taking a long sip of her coffee, Dani put the cup down and mouthed to Fred, "let's find that bug and speaker, partner."

It only took them a few minutes to find the other two devices. The bug was under a shelf, only three feet from where Brenda always sat to work on the computer. The tiny speaker was lying on the top shelf of the same shelving. In each case, Dani, wearing special gloves, bagged the devices for further testing in her lab. She was hoping for fingerprints.

"The camera and bug were positioned underneath the surface," Dani said, putting her tools away. "They were protected from dust particles. But, Brenda, that speaker has been there quite a while. It was very dusty."

Chapter 42

—•••—

BRENDA SAT IN FRONT of her computer monitor, her head in her hands. Fred walked up beside her, and, kneeling on one knee, he gently put his hand over her hand.

"Hey, Brenda, it's okay. Nobody's watching anymore. No one is listening."

Brenda slowly turned, looked into Fred's eyes. He could see the fear, the picture of several years past when a so-called friend tried to rape her. He could see the feeling of violation in her eyes. He stood, and taking her gently by the shoulders eased her to her feet. He wrapped his arms around her, holding her gently to his body. She willingly melted into his protective custody, resting her head on his chest.

Pulling back, she sank once again into her chair. Looking around the lab, floor to ceiling, wall to wall, a soft sigh escaped her lips. "I know you and Dani think you found all the devices, but my skin is still crawling."

"How about you and I get out of here for a couple of hours?" Fred asked. "It's almost dinner time—let's pick up some takeout and go to my place. We can brainstorm how this intrusion was pulled off."

"Sounds like a plan. I would like to get out of here, even if just for a little while. Let me call Russell, then we can go."

—•••—

Brenda sat quietly in the car, while Fred picked up several packages of Chinese dishes, egg rolls and wonton soup. He navigated to his house, hit the remote for the garage door, and parked the car. Fred grabbed their dinner off the back seat, and they entered the kitchen through the garage.

"I think a bottle of wine is in order, a nice nerve settler," Fred said, retrieving two wine goblets from the cupboard and a bottle of chardonnay from the refrigerator.

"Yes, that would be nice," Brenda whispered, looking out his sliding glass doors to the pond where several mallard ducks casually swam near the bank.

Fred handed her a glass of wine, and touching his to hers, he said, "Here's to getting the bastard."

A smile slowly crossed Brenda's face. "You are something else, Detective Watson. Are you always so caring to women in distress?"

"Only if she's gorgeous, and oh, yes, her last name has to be Kittles." Holding his glass carefully to the side, he leaned forward and tenderly brushed his lips over hers. Looking into her eyes he saw a wave of acceptance, of warmth. His heart beat faster, as he slowly put his glass down on the coffee table and lifted hers from her hand, setting it down beside his. Gently he took her in his arms and held her close.

She wrapped her arms around his neck and lifted her head with lips slightly parted, "Fred—"

"Shh," he sighed in a whisper. "You are so beautiful. I've wanted to hold you in my arms like this since the first time I saw you. If I move too fast, tell me. But, Brenda, when you're ready, I want to make love to you. I promise I'll stop, if you tell me to. But...I will never want to stop making love to you, now, or ever." He softly kissed her lips, a moan escaping from his constricted throat. Somehow he made himself pull back a little to make sure she was accepting his advances.

"Fred, I've never been with a man, but I know that wherever you're leading me, I'm ready to follow. My heart is beating so hard I can't catch my breath, yet I want to feel your lips on mine again. I want to feel them now."

He led her into his bedroom, and slowly undressed her. For each piece of clothing he carefully removed from her, he ripped one from his body. He couldn't believe the beauty of the woman standing in front of him. "I'll protect you forever, my love," he whispered, as he gently lifted her onto his bed.

Slowly, ever so slowly, he kissed her mouth, ran his hand down her arm, then under her chin and tenderly down her throat to her breasts. Her head eased back and her body rose to meet his hand as he slowly and gently explored her body. He knew she was ready to receive him, and God knew he was ready. He reached into the nightstand, fumbling with a packet. Protection in place, he slowly kissed her again, deeply. He didn't want to hurt her, he didn't want her to pull away, because he wanted to make love to this beautiful creature forever. As gently as he could, steeling himself not to lose control, he entered her. She instinctively grabbed his shoulders, clutching him to her, soft gasps escaping her mouth. He slowly brought them both to a place he never wanted to leave.

— ●●● —

Fred rolled away gathering her to him, both gasping for breath. He held her until her pulse slowed, and finally his slowed as well.

"Brenda, I'm falling in love with you. I'll wait for however long it takes for you to feel the same. I want you to know that somehow, someway, I want to be with you for the rest of my life. You don't have to respond now, but I had to tell you that my making love to you just now has been something I've dreamed about every time I've been with you."

— ●●● —

After a long warm shower together, and bundled in two of Fred's terrycloth bathrobes, they sat on the couch and finished their wine.

"I don't know about you, but I'm starving," Fred said. Getting up off the couch, he leaned down to kiss her tenderly. "I'll put that egg phooey and whatchamacallit in the microwave."

Brenda followed Fred into the kitchen. She helped him with the containers, set the napkins on the coffee table, and refilled their wine glasses. Sitting comfortably on the floor, leaning back against the couch eating their dinner with chopsticks, they talked about the devices they had found earlier in the day.

"First, I have to feel safe in the lab," Brenda said.

"I understand. Would it help if Dani installed an alarm under your desk? Something like a bank teller has? The alarm could buzz in Stone's office, Catherine's if you like, and also signal Dani at the department."

"I don't know about Catherine. I really wouldn't want to scare her, but, yes, I think the other two would be good. I now have your cell number programmed in my cell. If there's time, I'll call you first."

Fred could see that with the idea of being able to signal for help, Brenda was gaining her confidence back. She was beginning to think offensively, and her face became determined.

"That bastard," she said. "We have to get this creep before something bad happens. We have to set a trap."

Chapter 43

— • • • —

CHECKMATE! Brenda knew the game and felt ChessMan was ready to unleash his attack on the king. Another thing she knew for sure, there were at least two people involved—one on the outside of the company, and one on the inside. Only an insider would know about her new email address. What she didn't know was which one was the initiator, which one was pulling the strings, and which one was the master chess player.

She would take no more chances. She would stop hoping an outside agency would help. "Call us when you have more than a game of chess," her contact at Homeland Security as well as the Florida State police had said in response to her requests for help. "Send us your logbook. We'll take a look and see if our computer security guy can give you some tips," was another standard response.

She trusted only four people: Russell, Catherine, Fred, and of course, Captain Manny Salinas. They had to meet, but not in the company building. She now feared Russell's office was bugged, maybe even Catherine's. She quickly scribbled a note to them.

> "Russell, Catherine, I'm very concerned ChessMan is getting ready to attack. I believe he wants to bring the company down and, Russell, you may be in personal danger. Catherine, can we meet at your house in an hour—I'm afraid our offices may be bugged. Russell, nod if you want me to alert Captain Salinas and Fred about the meeting?
> Brenda"

Racing up the staircase to the third floor, she went to see Catherine first to be sure she agreed to host the meeting. Brenda went to her office but she wasn't there. Her assistant said she was in with the designers. Entering the design department, she spotted Catherine hunched over a blueprint.

"Catherine, I'm sorry to disturb you," Brenda said, handing Catherine her note.

"No problem," Catherine said, taking the note. Reading the message, Catherine looked up with alarm in her eyes. Anyone seeing the exchange would not have noticed any change in the women's demeanor, other than Catherine nodded in agreement with whatever Brenda had said. Catherine handed the note back to Brenda and seemingly went back to checking the plans in front of her.

Brenda then went to see Russell. "Hi, Maggie, is Russell in?"

Russell's office door was open and hearing Brenda ask for him, he called out, "Come on in, Brenda."

"Hi, Russell," she said, handing him the note.

"You're leaving your lab early this morning. What's this?" he asked, taking the note and reading the message.

"Yes, I can meet with you," he said, nodding in agreement.

"Thanks, Russell. See you later," Brenda said. She then went down to the first floor and out the lobby door. Walking around to the side of the building, she pulled out her cell phone and called Fred to let him know about the meeting. She asked if he could attend, and that Russell agreed it would be a good idea if Captain Salinas could join them.

Brenda then returned to the lab, opened her logbook, and glanced at yesterday's entry: "There was a camera, a bug and a speaker in my lab. Someone talked to me. He obviously could see me because he referenced where I was as I moved around. Detective Fred Watson and Sergeant Dani Trotter found and removed the devices."

She hastily wrote a new entry: "November 12. Meeting with Russell, Catherine, Fred and Captain Salinas at Catherine's house. Subject: Setting a trap for ChessMan."

Chapter 44

— • • • —

LUCY BREWED a fresh carafe of coffee and set it on the counter in Catherine's third-floor studio, the counter which usually held large blueprints. The meeting participants helped themselves to the coffee. Catherine picked up the glass of milk. They were quiet, no chitchat, as they readied to figure a way to stop a cyber attack, or worse, in its tracks.

The group turned to Brenda, faces stern, bodies sitting straight. Manny and Fred sat on one of the couches facing Russell, who sat in a chair next to Catherine.

Brenda stood and faced the group. "I believe ChessMan is ready to inflict serious damage to the company. As I see it, there are two areas that are the most likely targets. One, the millions of dollars in the project bank account. Two, the project design department, the intellectual property of the company destined to bring the multiplex to life."

"Brenda, we've been discussing this possibility for some time. Why do you feel there's imminent danger now, this morning?" Russell asked.

"Actually, it isn't all of a sudden. Yes, we've had several discussions over the last few months. But over the weekend it struck me that there seemed to be a confluence of events that made me think ChessMan is ready to strike."

Brenda paused, looked around the group seated in front of her, took a deep breath, and continued.

"Yesterday morning I found my lab had been compromised with a camera, a bug, and a speaker. Someone had been watching my every move, and listening to everything I said. Don't forget, Russell, several times when you came to the lab we discussed the events, and how to proceed. We telegraphed our actions. Question—how did someone get into my lab? How long had the camera and bug been there? Was it the doings of an inside person?"

"Because of the dust Dani found on the speaker," Fred said, "she believes the devices had been there awhile."

"Brenda, do you have a theory as to who the insider might be?" Catherine asked.

"Oh, there are several—Fatigate, Sitwell, or Balfor. Sanchez is a long shot, and. I don't think Vera is involved. As for the outsider, Victoria certainly comes to mind. However, she doesn't seem to have time to travel to Paris. But there may be more than one on the outside. After all, we're talking millions of dollars here."

"Brenda and I caught Fatigate and Standish having a little rendezvous in a bar on the beachside," Fred said. "Manny asked George to talk to Fatigate to find out what he was up to. Manny do you want to tell them what George found out?"

"Yes, I do. I've already talked to Russell about this. George went over to Fatigate's office the next day. When George asked him if he recognized any of the demonstrator's, he was vague at first. George pressed him, and he did confess that he had met one of them. He said that he and Victoria Standish had a mutual acquaintance and that this acquaintance suggested she meet with him. The acquaintance thought, if she played her cards right, she might be able to find out the construction schedule from Fatigate. She could then use the information to stage more demonstrations."

"So, did Jack give Victoria any information?" Catherine asked.

"He said he didn't, and he seemed quite irritated that she would ask him to divulge such information," Manny replied. "Russell, did Jack ever tell you about his meeting with Victoria, or George questioning him about it?"

"No, he didn't. After you told me about the meeting, I waited to see if he would, but he never said a word about knowing or meeting with her, or about George's visit."

"So, Brenda," Catherine said. "As Russell asked earlier, why the urgency today, this morning?"

"Today ChessMan started to explain the end game—capturing the king, bringing him down, putting him in checkmate. Because we discovered the camera and the other two pieces, ChessMan knows we are closing in on him, tightening security, and making it harder for him to penetrate the system. If he's going to attack, he has to do it soon. Also, given his chess game analogy, I believe Russell could be in danger—he *is* the king."

The implication of Brenda's ominous words hung in the air.

"I need to take a little break," Catherine said. "There's fresh coffee on the counter, and the restroom is on the other side of the bookcase. I'll ask Lucy to bring up some fruit and a few sandwiches. Then, my friends, we'll put our heads together and see if we can't come up with a plan to win this game. I can see by Brenda's face, that she already has a scheme in mind."

The group stood, stretched their legs, and walked in different directions. Fred joined Brenda, who was topping off her coffee cup.

"Are you okay?" he asked, quietly.

She looked up at him with her dark eyes. He could see the worry, but also her determination. "Yes, I'm okay. I just want to get this bastard before he gets Russell, or the company, or, God forbid, both."

—•••—

The group reassembled, refreshed and ready to hear Brenda's ideas.

"Tell us your plan, Brenda," Russell said. "How can we stop this attack?"

"When we leave here today, I'll again change the system manager's user ID and password, however, this time I'll set an alert so I'll know if someone tries to get into the system files, but more on that in a minute."

"Okay," Russell, said, "but how about the bank account?"

"I've already talked to our bank manager about setting up a dummy account with several million virtual-dollars in it—nothing real. I'm also asking for your okay, Russell, to bring Vera into our group, on a need-to-know basis."

Brenda paused, taking a sip of coffee, and then again addressing the group. "Now, for the trap! I will leave the door open, so to speak—the login access to the bank account, the same route ChessMan took when he logged in before. But now, a new program command will automatically reroute the intruder, with any attempt to withdraw or wire transfer funds, to the virtual phony account. From the outside, all will appear like banking as usual, accepting new deposits and commands from Vera. The bank will recognize Vera's login to pay bills using a biometric pad, recognition of her fingerprint. Her login will go to the real account."

"Have any of the computer breaches been leaked outside of the three of you?" Manny asked.

"I haven't heard anyone talking about our computer system being comprised, have you, Catherine?" Russell asked.

"No. Several have complained about the frequent changing of their passwords, but they seem to be chalking it up to Brenda's paranoia about computer security," Catherine said smiling at Brenda.

"As I said," Brenda continued, "we have to bring Vera into the loop. She must be read into the trap, using some police terminology." Brenda exchanged smiles with Fred. It was the first time since the meeting had started that she seemed to relax.

"Now, there's one more thing I have to address with you," Brenda said. "It has to do with the alert mechanism I mentioned earlier. The software program I used to trace the emails back to Paris, Bern, and to Zurich, has an alert component that I will set. Whenever the CAD files, or the bogus bank account, are accessed from an outside computer, even if it is legitimate, such as one of Catherine's design team members logging in from home, I will receive an alert. It will also be set to trigger if an email lands in an inbox from an anonymous sender, no matter to whom it is addressed."

"What happens when the alert is triggered?" Catherine asked.

"The alert is in the form of a text message, and a beep from my cell phone, as well as triggering the printer in the lab to print every keystroke ChessMan types—no more sweeping away his tracks. This alert is live 24/7. The printed record can be used as evidence. This trigger, of course, will capture legitimate logins as well. My job is to check each alert and find the one that is illegitimate. I will know instantly when and from where ChessMan is lurking."

"Well, I say let's give your trap a go, Brenda," Russell said. "Please go ahead and talk to Vera. I'll call her from here, before I leave, to tell her that you must see her today. I hope your assumptions are wrong, but I'm afraid you're right."

"If I'm right, I believe ChessMan will make his move to checkmate soon. If I'm wrong, I'll take the first plane out of here that's heading to Alaska with my tail between my legs."

Chapter 45

—•••—

MANNY AGREED with Brenda that an attack seemed imminent. Someone was going to get hurt. But who? Why? What was ChessMan after? Was it to stop the construction of the multiplex development from going forward, and, if so, was Victoria Standish the leader of this deadly game of cyber crime? Had she become aligned with ChessMan? Was *she* ChessMan? Or, were Victoria's threats to Stone, and ChessMan's intrusion into the company's computer, two separate capers that just happened to occur at the same time?

Peaches settled down on her pillow by Manny's desk, head down between her paws, but her eyes continued to follow her master pacing up and down from his desk to the electronic whiteboard. Several times in the last hour he pulled a cigarette from his left breast pocket, only to jam it back. He patted his left and right pants pocket, looking for his Nicorette gum. He quickly unwrapped a fresh piece and put it in his mouth. He had cut his scotch-on-the-rocks down to two drinks a night. He had done this by keeping the image of Catherine and her unborn child in the forefront of his mind. On the other hand, quitting his smoking habit had remained elusive at best.

Manny knelt down giving Peaches a loving scratch behind her ears. Peaches nudged his hand in return. Manny was looking at his best friend, but his mind only saw a parade of suspects flash one by one in front of his eyes. Computer hacking is a crime, but murder was eligible for the death penalty in Florida.

"Hey, captain, we brought you a cup of coffee, but I see from the wastebasket you have already enjoyed some morning caffeine," Dani said, setting a fresh cup on his desk with the compulsory extra creamers and sugar packets. Following on her heels were Manny's two detectives.

"Thanks for the coffee, Dani. It's nice and hot," Manny said.

Fred opened a large brown envelope and withdrew four pieces of paper. "Here are copies of Victoria's email to Stone that he told us about yesterday." Handing everyone a copy, he continued, "There sure seems to be an escalation from peaceful demonstration to potential violence in her case. As you can see, she's making veiled threats. I say veiled because we don't know exactly what she means by...*will stop you,* or *we will cease construction for you.*"

"George, go talk to her again," Manny ordered. "See if you can find out what she has in mind. Ask her how she knew about the laying of the cornerstone. Was it from Fatigate? And ask her if she plays chess. Even if she and ChessMan haven't joined up yet, they could in the future. Fred, call Brenda to see if her plans to trap ChessMan in the act are in place. While you do that, I'll fill George and Dani in on what S&A's canny computer scientist came up with to trap the bastard."

— • • • —

Fred returned with fresh coffee for the team. "Brenda said everything is set up and operational as we speak," he said, handing out the cups.

"George, what about Balfor, Sanchez, and Fatigate?" Manny asked, chewing hard on a fresh chiclet of gum. "Ouch. Damn. I bit the inside of my mouth." He rubbed his tongue over the sore and then took a sip of coffee.

"Fatigate's only been with Stone for awhile," George reported. "He knows tons about negotiating to get the best price on goods and labor. He's a hands-on kind of guy and uses his computer extensively, as does Balfor. I don't see a motive for either of them. Of course, the money that's pouring into the company, and the millions to come, would give Snow White a motive."

"ChessMan repeatedly refers to capturing the king," Manny said. "Bringing him down. If the real target is Stone and the money, then there's someone else who could be pulling the strings—Douglas Bradshaw."

"But, Manny," Dani interrupted, "Bradshaw's in prison waiting for trial."

"He wouldn't be the first prisoner who tried to get even with someone, and don't forget, he hates Stone's guts. Fred, check with the jail and find out who Bradshaw's visitors are. Also, stop in to see Sanchez again. See if he knows more about computers than he's letting on. Let's regroup at five this afternoon, and for God's sake, bring me some answers."

Chapter 46

—•••—

RUSSELL STOOD at the picture window in his office, lost in thought, when Catherine walked in.

"Hello, Russell. It's a lovely morning isn't it?"

"Yes, it is, Catherine. Thank you for coming. I know you're busy with the designs, but I felt I had to see you. A couple of months ago I talked to you about a partnership in Stone & Associates. You said you'd think about it."

"Yes. I've given it a lot of thought."

"After the meeting at your house, the seriousness and potential danger the company is in, I'm asking you for your answer. I have an obligation to all the businesses and investors who have given their money, and even their reputations to make the multiplex project a success. If something should happen to me, I want to be sure my successor is in place to see the project to fruition."

"I understand, Russell, and I've thought about the ramifications to the development if something should happen to the company, or, God forbid, to you."

"I want to legally add you as a full partner with the stipulation that should anything happen to me, where I can't continue as president, that you are to assume the office and all the responsibilities that go with it. I'm not asking you to front any money, or buy the partnership. I feel you've earned it."

"Russell, you aren't thinking of retiring now, are you, because—"

"No no. As I told you before, I would hand over the operation to you after the baby is born, and you feel you're ready. That part of our conversation is strictly between the two of us. However, the announcement, that you are a full partner, I would like to make as soon as the documents are drawn up and signed. The papers will also contain the succession plan, just in case it's needed. What do you say, Catherine? Will you accept a partnership in Stone & Associates?"

"Yes, Russell, I will be honored to accept a partnership in Stone & Associates."

Chapter 47

— • • • —

CATHERINE LEFT work early, overwhelmed by Russell's offer of a partnership and his succession plan. She wanted some extra time to get ready for a dinner out with Manny. He was taking her to the beautiful restaurant at the North Shore Resort hotel. She lingered in the warmth of her bubble bath, the bubbles now surrounding her enlarged belly. Other than a month of sporadic morning sickness, her pregnancy had proceeded as Mother Nature planned. The baby was an active little guy—she could see him kicking the bubbles circling his cocoon.

Carefully stepping out of the tub, she toweled off and went into her dressing room. Earlier in the week she had purchased a black dress for special occasions. The black sequined top, with slender straps, fell just below her non-existent waistline, and, from underneath the sparkling top, a skirt of filmy black chiffon fell softly to her knees. A pair of black strappy heels finished the ensemble. Hearing the doorbell ring, she left her bedroom and stood at the top of her winding staircase. Lucy answered the door and invited Manny to come inside.

"Now there is a vision," he said, looking up at Catherine. Her blonde hair fell in soft waves to her shoulders, showcasing her radiant brown eyes and full dusty-rose pink lips.

"The ever gallant captain. I've been looking forward to our night out," she said, carefully descending the staircase.

Manny put his hands on her shoulders and softly kissed both of her cheeks, and then held her out at arm's length. "I've been looking forward to tonight as well," he said beaming. He took the light wrap from her hand and draped it around her shoulders. The

November evening air was cool, now that the mild heat of the day had dissipated.

"We're leaving, Lucy," Catherine called out over her shoulder as they went out the door.

— ••• —

Driving to the ocean side of Daytona Beach, Manny chatted about the upcoming holidays. He left conversation about the case for another time. Pulling up under the portico of the resort, Manny helped Catherine out of the car and handed the keys to the valet. They walked through the spacious white marble lobby to the elegant dining room overlooking a patio and on out to the ocean. An abundance of candles provided a soft glow, an inviting ambiance to the room.

Manny pulled the white upholstered chair out for Catherine. Even with her obviously pregnant frame, she gracefully took the seat he offered.

"I feel as if I'm in the presence of royalty. You look so beautiful tonight, Cat. Pregnancy becomes you. How is the little guy treating you?"

"He's definitely going to be an athlete the way he kicks."

"What would you like this evening, my dear?" Manny asked. He didn't catch the smile she gave him. It was the first time he had used a term of endearment with her. When she didn't answer, he looked up at her and saw the warmth in her eyes.

"You know, I believe I'll have a small glass of wine. I've been very good at skipping alcohol, but this is such a special night out. I think little Stephen can handle it."

"Okay. What do you fancy for dinner, and then we'll make the wine selection?"

"I'll have the swordfish and for wine, instead of white, I'd like a glass of merlot, please. That way I can provide some nutritional value. At least that's what they say about red wine."

"Swordfish it is, but I think I'll treat myself to a steak." Manny gave their order to the waiter, along with crab cakes as an appetizer. The young man left and soon returned with the wine.

Enjoying the glow of the candle and the richness of the wine, Manny reached into his pocket and drew out a small, long velvet box. "I bought you a gift, Cat. I hope you like it," he said, setting the box in front of her.

"Manny, I love presents, but you really shouldn't have."

"Hey, you haven't seen it yet. Maybe there's a string of macaroni in that box."

"Somehow I doubt it." Catherine opened the black-velvet case to reveal an exquisite bracelet—three strands of pearls, with a white-gold filigree clasp fashioned to catch the light. "Manny, this is beautiful. Please help me put it on," she said, leaning over to give him a kiss on his cheek.

He fastened the clasp and held her hand up, admiring how it looked on her wrist. He then lifted her hand and kissed the top of her slender fingers.

A single tear slid out of the corner of her eye, she quickly dabbed it with her napkin. "Thank you...it's lovely. Now you've got me all teary eyed. Excuse me a minute while I freshen up."

Catherine returned to the table and for the rest of the dinner held her hand in a position so she could admire the bracelet—her wrist on the table, or holding her wine glass at an angle so the clasp twinkled in the candlelight.

"Manny, I've had a funny feeling that someone was watching us during dinner. Did you feel it?"

"Actually, I did once. My eyes were drawn to my left, about three tables over. A middle-aged man was looking our way, but when I glanced over again he was gone. I felt it just before our coffee was served. Did you see anyone you knew?"

"No. I first felt it when our wine was served. I gazed around the room but didn't notice anyone staring at us. I do remember the man you describe, but when I looked in his direction, he seemed to be engrossed in the menu. I'm sure it was nothing."

"Well, I for one don't want anyone intruding in our evening," Manny said, with a smile.

Chapter 48

—•••—

MANNY AND PEACHES were awakened with the December sun peeking up over the horizon filling his bedroom with its cool rays. Even though it had been a couple of weeks since his dinner with Catherine, he still wore a smile on his face remembering the evening. He and Peaches jumped off the aft-deck of his houseboat and took their morning jog. As his feet pounded the pavement, he also mulled over the Stone case. Construction was proceeding without incident. Brenda's warning that ChessMan would make a move soon hadn't panned out. No events had occurred since she set the trap.

Returning to the houseboat, Peaches ate the cup of dog food in her bowl. Manny took a quick shower, fixed a cup of coffee to go, and headed into the department. When he walked into the bullpen he felt as if everything was right with the world, his world anyway. Peaches plopped down on her pillow just as Manny's phone rang.

"Salinas here...what the hell are you saying, George?" Manny barked into the phone.

"Bradshaw escaped from the courthouse," George shouted back rushing his words. "He was being escorted to the courtroom for a change-of-venue appeal. It all came down in the hall. The guard was the only person with him. He evidently removed the shackles from Bradshaw's wrists and ankles, and was either overpowered by Bradshaw, or the guard gave him his gun. Bradshaw shot him and ran out of the building to a waiting car. I'm sure someone bought the guard off to help Bradshaw escape and now he's dead. Bradshaw escaped so fast that no one could catch up with the fleeing car. We don't know who the driver is, and we don't know where Bradshaw is."

"Did you call in an APB on him?" Manny shouted, chewing, pacing, and planning his next move.

"Fred called it in," George said, still talking rapidly. "We're in separate cars, cruising the streets around the courthouse to see if we can spot the vehicle. A bystander saw a man in an orange jumpsuit climb into a black Ford SUV, but he didn't get anything on the plate."

"Okay," Manny said. "Given the guy's a pilot he may try to fly out of our reach. I'll alert the airports and set up roadblocks on Route 1, A1A, and Route 95, north and south. If he tries any of these routes, we'll get him unless he goes underground."

"The courthouse isn't far from Stone & Associates," George said clipping his words off.

"I'll notify Russell Stone and Catherine Hainsworth," Manny said, as he continued to pace in the bullpen. "Call me if you get any news on him." Manny cut the connection. He immediately dialed Stone & Associates, and Maggie put him through to Russell.

"Russell, bad news. Bradshaw just escaped and is on the loose. Russell, he's armed. Be careful. I'm sending over a couple of officers to stake out your building. I suggest you not go wandering around town until we find the bastard."

"Sounds like a good suggestion," Russell said. "Let me know if you get a lead on him."

"Russell, has Cat come into work yet?"

"I haven't seen her. She usually stops by to say hello on her way to her office."

"Please check. I'll call her house."

—•••—

"Cat, I'm glad you're still home," Manny said.

"Hey, you don't sound good. What's happening?"

"I'm calling with bad news. Bradshaw just pulled off an escape at the courthouse. I'm a little concerned for your safety. Given your involvement in the case when he murdered Julie Stone, I don't know what this nut might do. Can you stay home for awhile? I'll let you know as soon as we catch him. But until then I'll feel better if you don't go into work today."

"Oh, Manny. That's awful. Yes, of course, I'll stay home and lock the doors, and load that pistol I bought. He'd better not come near me."

"I'm going to send an officer to your house to be on the safe side. I've already alerted Russell, and a couple of officers are on their way over to the company. Ask Lucy to help you lock up, and both of you stay inside until I let you know he's been arrested."

Chapter 49

—•••—

BRENDA DIDN'T FIX her normal cup of coffee, opting instead to stop at a coffee shop on the way to work. She was on edge. She hadn't slept all night, tossing and turning, going to the kitchen for a cup of chamomile tea, taking an aspirin. Nothing helped.

The side door to Stone & Associates was still locked, so she went in through the front entrance, to the elevator, and down to her lab. Flicking on the light, she looked apprehensively at her monitor. *Thank God,* she thought. The screen was blank.

She set her briefcase, and the few folders she had taken home, down by the lab door. Sipping her coffee, she walked to her chair in front of the monitor and logged into her email. She read her messages, replying to those that required an answer, and then checked the system log file. Nothing unusual happened in the seven hours since she last checked. The printer tray was empty—no alerts.

At 10:30, and with a fresh cup of coffee and a muffin from the vending machines, she checked her email again. Her screen instantly filled with a message from anonymous.

> *"Good morning, Brenda.*
> *This is my last chess tutorial. I hope you are following the rules closely.*
> *The king can move in any direction, but, poor fellow, he can move only one square at a time. When he is cornered, with no one to protect him, he has no defense. He is shackled. Trapped. There is no escape. Game over! CHECKMATE!*

Goodbye"

Brenda stared at the message. ChessMan's words screamed out of the monitor at her—shackled, trapped, no escape. CHECKMATE! The printer quickly finished printing the message—the anonymous email automatically triggering the print command. Her coffee and muffin forgotten, she grabbed her cell phone and punched Fred's code.

Fred answered on the first ring. "Hi, Brenda. What's up?" he said breathing rapidly into the mouthpiece.

"Fred, I just got a message threatening checkmate. Fred, I'm sure something awful is going to happen today."

"Yes, well it already has. Sorry, I've gotta run. Bradshaw just overpowered his guard and got away. He was about to enter the courtroom for a hearing when it happened. He shot the guard and fled. However, someone was waiting for him because a car was seen squealing away from the courthouse."

"Oh, God. Keep me posted."

"You, too. Call me if you get any more messages. Brenda, keep your door locked. Bradshaw's armed."

Brenda closed her cell. Two seconds later it let out a beep. She flipped it open. It was the automatic alert. Someone had just accessed the accounting space on the system. Reigning in her nerves, she sat in front of her monitor, hand on the mouse. She clicked a few icons to enter the computer as system manager. From this vantage point she could monitor everything and everyone on the system. She heard her printer valiantly capturing each keystroke the intruder typed.

Brenda activated the tracing program, and within seconds she had the location of the incoming line he was using and the address. She couldn't believe her eyes. Brenda grabbed her lab telephone and dialed the number for Tillie's cyber café.

"House of Beads and Cyber Café, may I help you," Tillie answered.

"Tillie, this is Brenda Kittles." She knew she was speaking fast, her breathing ragged.

"Oh, yes, hello Bren—"

"Tillie, is your cyber café open?"

"Why, yes it is and Pete is—"

"Tillie, please ask Pete to pick up. It's an emergency."

"Yes. Okay. Right away."

Brenda could hear Tillie calling to Pete, walking, taking the phone to him. Waiting for Pete to pick up, Brenda pulled out her cell phone and selected Fred's number.

Fred came on the phone at the same time Pete said hello. Holding both phones to her ears, Brenda in an urgent voice said, "Fred, Daytona Pete is on my other phone at the House of Beads' cyber café. Pete, is there anybody at your computer station C7?"

"Yes, there's a man. He's been here only about ten or so minutes. Why?" Pete asked.

"Fred, he's ChessMan," Brenda said.

"Tell Pete to watch him. Do not engage. I'm only three minutes away," Fred said, and hung up.

"Pete," Brenda said, "I just spoke with Detective Watson. He asks that you watch the man. Do not engage. He'll be at the shop in a few minutes. Pete, don't interrupt this man, but if he gets up to leave try to detain him. Whatever you do, don't make him think anything is wrong."

—•••—

Pete handed the phone back to Tillie and asked her to go back into the bead side of the shop. "Detective Watson will be arriving any minute," he said quietly. "Please prop the shop door open for him and stay by the door."

Pete went behind the small counter in the cyber café and shuffled some papers around. He saw the squad car pull up in front of the shop. Fred and another officer got out of the car and came in the front entrance. Pete looked over at the man in the corner on station C7. He looked irritated. His face in a deep scowl.

Fred walked in and followed Pete's gesture to the computer in the back corner.

"What are you doing there, my friend?" Fred asked, forcibly lifting the man out of his chair, slamming him against the wall, and cuffing him. Fred looked down at the monitor.

"Transfer request denied. Insufficient funds!"

"Pete, can you capture this screen for me?" Fred asked, over his shoulder. "I need you to save the words."

The cuffed man cursed and squirmed, trying to get free. The officer with Fred forced the man to the floor, shackled his ankles. Fishing in the man's pockets, Fred pulled out his driver's license.

"Well, Mr. Philip Longwood, you have some explaining to do. You are under arrest for the illegal use of the internet, illegally entering a corporate bank account with the intent to remove funds, and for committing cyber espionage. That's just for starters. You have the right to remain silent and to refuse to answer any questions. Anything you do or say may be used against you in a court of law. Do you understand?"

"Ya, ya," Longwood yelled as he continued to struggle. "I didn't do anything wrong, you shitheads. You can't prove a thing,"

"Oh, really? That's what you think. Get him in the car," Fred barked to the other officer. Chuckling, "I believe this is where Brenda would say 'Checkmate'. I have a call to make." Fred punched in Brenda's cell-phone code.

"Brenda, we got him," Fred said.

"What's his name?"

"His driver's license says he's Philip Longwood."

"I've heard that name before, but I can't remember where. "What's happening with Bradshaw?"

"He's still on the loose. Manny called Russell and Catherine to alert them that he might, just might, try to find them," Fred said. "We have an APB out for him. As soon as we get this Longwood guy to the department, I'm heading over to you. In the meantime, keep that lab door locked."

Chapter 50

—•••—

THE BLACK SUV had tinted windows—no one could see the occupants, or that one wore an orange jumpsuit. The automobile made a sharp turn down a residential, tree-lined street. Turning sharply into a driveway, the vehicle ducked into an open garage. The driver cut the engine, clicked the garage door button, and the black bat was safely out of sight in its cave. Bradshaw thanked the driver, jumped out, and entered the house. He needed a shower and a shave in the worst way.

Standing in the shower he let the grime of prison wash down the drain. Street clothes were laid out on the bed, as well as a gray wig, mustache, bushy eyebrows, and very dark sunglasses. Donning the disguise, he stood back and examined the results in the mirror.

"Hey, Douglas, you look different. No one will recognize you. Now let's get going," the driver said, standing in the doorway of the bedroom.

"I'm with you, let's get going," Bradshaw repeated. "You said that Stone was in his office when you left?"

"That's right. I'm sure he'll be surprised to see you."

—•••—

The driver started the engine of a gray sedan parked next to the black SUV. Bradshaw climbed into the passenger seat and the sedan emerged from the garage. The garage door closed as the sedan pulled into the street, heading to Stone and Associates. Turning into the parking lot, the driver pulled the car into a space marked Visitor.

"I'll meet you back here in thirty minutes. Synchronize your watch with mine. I have 11:36," Bradshaw said.

"Check," the driver replied. "The stairs down to the computer lab will be the first door on your left after you pass the receptionist. You have the new code. Brenda Kittles will be there."

Douglas emerged from the car and nonchalantly made his way to the front of the building. He entered the lobby, nodded to the receptionist, turned the corner out of view and opened the door to the stairwell. Entering the basement hallway, he stopped at the la

b door. The hall was clear. He punched in the code and entered the lab. Brenda was at her desk checking the system log. She heard the door open, but didn't look up, thinking it was Russell.

"Russell, I have some more data to show you," she said.

Douglas grabbed her from behind placing his hand over her mouth and the gun the guard had given him to her head.

"Now, Miss Kittles, just do as I say and no one will get hurt. Pick up the phone and call Stone. No funny moves. Tell him you need to see him in the lab. You have something important to show him. You got that?"

Brenda nodded her head that she understood. She did as the man with the gun instructed—punched in Russell's number.

"Hi, Brenda," Russell said, seeing her caller ID "What's up?"

"Russell, can you come down to the lab? I have something important to show you."

"Sure, I'll be right down."

"That was very good, Miss Kittles," Bradshaw said. "Now get up. We're going over behind that rack of equipment to your left." He maneuvered Brenda in front of him, still holding her in a vice-like grip. Two minutes later, the door's lock release clicked, and Russell entered the lab. The door automatically swung shut behind him.

"Brenda, are you here?" Russell called.

"Yes, she's here, Russell." Bradshaw stepped out from behind the wall of equipment, Brenda in front of him, the gun still pressed against her head.

"Who are you?" Russell asked. "What are you doing here?"

"Oh, now, Russy. You mean to tell me you don't recognize your old buddy? I'm hurt."

"Douglas?"

Brenda could see recognition entering Russell's eyes, then alarm.

"I heard you were on the run," Russell said, eyes darting around the lab. "Rather stupid to come here isn't it? You'll never be able to leave. We've all been alerted to watch for you."

"Well, they aren't doing a very good job are they? I just waltzed in here easy as you please. I've had plenty of time to plan for today, locked in that smelly cramped cell, men yelling, crying, screaming. Very unpleasant. Once I take care of my unfinished business, disposing of you once and for all, I have a rendezvous with ten-million dollars so I can live happily ever after. Miss Kittles, you were very clever at tracking down the culprit who hacked into your computer system. Unfortunately for you, he was always a step ahead."

Bradshaw removed his hand from her mouth so Brenda could speak. "I heard you were cunning, Mr. Bradshaw, but you were behind bars. You had to have inside help. Who helped you, Mr. Bradshaw?" Brenda hissed.

"Now, now, Miss Kittles. You're telling me I couldn't magically appear, get into your computer, and leave messages on your monitor?"

"As long as you know the sequence of ones and zeroes, a person can pretty much command a computer to do his bidding," Brenda said, "but you have to know the code. Of course, you can always guess, and there are programs to automatically try millions of sequences to save you time, but I doubt prison would have afforded you such sophisticated software." As Brenda talked, she inched closer to her desk drawer, the one with the gun. Loaded.

"You're right, Miss Kittles. One needs to have certain information. But we're wasting time. I only have five more minutes until my next stop, so, Russell, it's time for you to say bye bye and join your pretty wife, Julie. I was sorry I didn't get a chance to see her after she drank the champagne cocktail I gave her. But, you,

Russell, I will watch you die. All the years you won the prizes instead of me, but this time I will get the prize, the money you worked so hard to acquire."

Douglas didn't notice that Brenda had slowly moved away from him. She was now in arms reach of the drawer, the drawer where she had put her revolver. She was also just inches from the button that would shut down the server, crashing the system. Glancing at Bradshaw out of the corner of her eye, she slowly moved her hand to the system's power switch. She pressed the button. She then moved her hand to the drawer and slowly opened it enough to see the cloth that covered the gun. She knew Fred was on his way, but would he get here in time? *Please, dear God, let someone come down to see why the server crashed,* she thought.

"So, Russell, any last words you want to say before joining your wife?" Douglas asked.

Russell could see Brenda drifting off to Douglas's left. He didn't know what she planned, but he did know her options were better than his.

The door's keypad clicked and Ben and Fred entered the room. Fred immediately took in the situation and pushed Ben to the floor landing on top of him.

Startled, Bradshaw swung his gun in Fred's direction.

Brenda pulled the gun out of the drawer.

"Drop—"

"Never—"

Shots rang out.

Russell fell back against the wall.

Bradshaw crumpled to the ground, his gun falling from his fingers.

Brenda stood frozen, splattered with Bradshaw's blood, both hands molded to her pistol. She had just shot a man in the back.

Fred immediately called for medical assistance to Stone & Associates. A man had been shot. He checked Douglas for a pulse. There was none. It was then he saw Russell leaning against the wall, a bloodstain growing larger on the shoulder of his shirt. He had been hit with the first bullet Bradshaw squeezed off before Brenda's bullet brought him down.

"Russell," Fred said, easing Stone into a chair, "medics are on the way. Hang on?" Fred tore his own shirt off using it as a compress on Russell's wound to stem the flow of blood.

"Yes, I'll be okay," Russell said, grimacing, holding Fred's shirt to his shoulder. "Go help Brenda."

Fred slowly walked to the traumatized woman, carefully removing the gun from her hand. Putting the gun down on the computer table he took her in his arms, slowly rocking her back and forth.

"It's okay, baby. It's okay. You did good. You saved Russell's life."

Brenda began to tremble. Fred held her tighter, still rocking. "Baby, you're okay. Everything's okay."

Brenda not budging from the comfort of Fred's arms finally spoke. "I was so scared he was going to shoot Russell. And then you came in. Fred, you were in his line of fire. I had to act. Thank God, I had the gun in my desk. Fred, wonder if—"

"*If* wasn't in the cards today, my love."

Again the click of the lab door was heard. Vera and Manny rushed in.

"Well this is a heck of a scene," Manny said, his eyebrows drawn together. He went to the dead man on the floor. Manny carefully pulled at the man's hair—it slid off in his hand. Unclipping his cell from his belt, he called Sam at the morgue. "Sam you'll never guess who we have here—Douglas Bradshaw, a dead Douglas Bradshaw. Bring over the wagon to Stone & Associates. Come to the side entrance, where you picked up the last body, by the dumpster. An officer will be waiting at the door to let you in." Closing his cell, he turned to Sitwell. "Ben, can you get that door open?"

"Uh, sure," Ben said, still shaken by what had just taken place.

It was only then that Manny saw Russell, his blood-soaked shirt sticking to his body, his face ashen, full of pain. Kneeling in front of him he asked, in a soft but insistent voice, "Russell, does anyone on your staff drive a black SUV?"

Russell looked at Manny, not comprehending what he had asked.

Fred released his hold on Brenda. She knelt beside Russell, quickly gaining her composure. "Russell, someone inside helped Bradshaw," Brenda said. "He may be driving that car."

"Balfor and Sanchez," Vera piped up. "They both have big black cars."

"Fred, check to see if Balfor is in the building," Manny ordered. "If he is, take him in for questioning. If not, put out an APB on him. I'll call the department to have an officer pick up Sanchez."

Fred leaned down and kissed the top of Brenda's head, "I'll see you later, baby. Sure you're okay?" he asked, whispering in her ear.

"Yes, I'm okay. Come see me when you're free from catching the bad guys," she said, trying to smile and then turning back to Russell. Both she and Manny eased Russell out of the chair, helping him to lie down on the floor.

Fred walked to the lab door and opened it just as George shoved Balfor into the room, handcuffed. "Look who I found sitting in a car in the parking lot with the motor running."

"You've made a terrible mistake," Balfor yelled at George struggling to free himself. "I'm going to sue the whole goddamn police department for false arrest," he screamed. Everyone looked at him, understanding that he was the one, the insider, who gave all the secret IDs and passwords to the hacker, to ChessMan. Seeing the disgust and hatred in Russell's pained eyes, Balfor collapsed, breaking into racking sobs. "He was going to give me a lot of money," he said through his sobs," He promised if I helped him, I would live like a prince for the rest of my life."

Chapter 51

— • • • —

TEN DAYS HAD PASSED since Bradshaw's death and the arrest of Longwood and Balfor. It was time to celebrate. Catherine decided a holiday dinner party would be perfect. She scheduled the celebration on a Sunday, just five weeks prior to her due date.

She and Brenda took Friday off, and, with Lucy's help plus three high school girls, they turned the inside and outside of the house into a holiday of lights, sounds, and scents that rivaled Disney World, just an hour away. Catherine and Brenda intertwined boxwood boughs with tiny white lights, and then fished the garlands through the spindles of the curved staircase to the third floor. Fred came over, and he and Brenda strung lights outside, under Catherine's supervision and watchful eye. Lucy baked up a storm, filling the kitchen table and counter with cooling delicacies. The lighting crew often asked for Lucy's opinion as a ruse to sample her treats.

— • • • —

Everyone was relaxed and in a festive holiday mood. The guests climbed the two flights of stairs to Catherine's design studio and were greeted by an enormous twelve-foot Christmas tree standing in the center of the window wall, sparkling with an abundance of tiny white lights.

Fred was in charge of the music, with orders from Catherine that he could choose anything he liked as long as it was seasonal music peppered with good old fashioned carols.

Catherine greeted Manny when he arrived. He lifted her hand and kissed the top of her slender fingers. She reciprocated with a tender kiss on his cheek. She was wearing the same sparkling top and chiffon skirt she wore when they last went out to dinner. Catherine held up her wrist, so he could admire the bracelet he had given her.

"Manny, bring Peaches into the kitchen so I can show her the bowl I set out for her treats."

In the kitchen, all seemed to be organized chaos. Catherine showed Peaches her dish, already holding a tasty piece of dinner roll slathered with liver pate. "Lucy, can I borrow Wendy for a few minutes? I'm going on up to the studio with Manny, but Russell isn't here yet so I'd like her to greet him. He should be here soon."

— • • • —

Manny tended bar, but after the first round people seemed happy to replenish their own drinks. It wasn't long before the conversation centered on ChessMan and Douglas Bradshaw.

Vera asked Manny how the murdered cleaner fit into the scheme.

"Well, first of all much has happened in the last ten days," Manny said.

Everyone heard Vera's question and quickly congregated in the client sitting area. Manny's team knew the whole story, but the others only bits and pieces.

"Longwood and Balfor have turned on each other, and, of course, with Bradshaw out of the picture, they each felt an opportunity to lay all the blame on him. In the beginning, it seems every time Longwood, Bradshaw's former CFO, visited him in jail, Bradshaw complained how he wanted to get Russell. Bradshaw became consumed with his hatred for Russell," Manny said, tilting his head with a questioning look at Russell to see if he minded the story coming out. Russell nodded to go ahead. "They conjectured that the one thing that would hurt Russell the most was to bring the company down—hack into the bank account and steal the money after the majority of the funds had been deposited."

"By that time," Russell said, "deposits had topped twenty-million dollars."

"The whole idea of losing all that money scared me to death, I can tell you," Vera said, looking up at her husband who patted her hand.

"Who knew how to hack into the bank account—Balfor?" Fatigate asked.

"Well, Longwood is somewhat computer savvy," Manny continued, "so he thought he could handle the job, but he immediately ran into login and password issues. Brenda knew her stuff, and Longwood hit a brick wall, a virtual brick wall." Everyone smiled at the comment, looking over at Brenda. She was not smiling, and gave a shake of her head, no way.

"Then according to Longwood, he and Bradshaw knew they had to enlist someone on the inside, someone who really knew how to get around the system, and where to find the password file. I guess they concentrated on the login information for Russell, Catherine, Vera, and Brenda. Doing some digging, there were only two who might give them the information they needed—Balfor and our friend, Jack Fatigate here."

"I wish they had approached me," Fatigate said. "I would've given them the what for, and I would have been on your doorstep, Russell, in two seconds flat."

"Yes, well, that's probably why they didn't choose you," Manny said. "They sensed you had developed a bond with Russell and were loyal to him. Balfor, on the other hand, was a very different story. He was chosen because his early work experience was installing networks and progressed to an intimate knowledge of project software. But gambling was his Achilles heel. He was a regular customer at the poker club, part of the Daytona Beach dog track. He was into them for thousands of dollars."

"Did Balfor tell you this, or did Longwood?" Sitwell asked.

"Longwood. But, we checked the story with the poker parlor, and it panned out. Longwood approached Balfor, seeking his cooperation. Balfor, seeing a way to pay his gambling debt, agreed to help. Help, that is, for twenty-five percent of the take. They tested Balfor—he gave them Russell's login and password to his office PC. Longwood says he went to a motel one night, very late, to try the codes Balfor had given him to get into Russell's account. Longwood succeeded. That was all he did the first time—in and out."

"So that wasn't the login to the bank?" Russell asked, his arm in a sling, his eyes concentrating on Manny.

"No, that was later," Manny said. "Then the criminal mind, with acute paranoia, set in, and they made their first mistake. Longwood convinced Bradshaw that they should monitor Brenda's reaction to what was happening with the system. Test her. Maybe she wouldn't notice. Excuse me, that was their first mistake, thinking she wouldn't notice."

Again everyone smiled at Brenda, some chuckled. This time, Brenda joined them.

"They decided to plant a camera, a bug and a speaker in her lab. So they had to get in, but they also didn't want Balfor to know about the devices. They thought if he ratted on them to Brenda, they would hear and see him tell her. Longwood staked out the building for several nights. Every night, a cleaning man dumped trash into the side dumpster. Each time he pulled out a key to get back in."

"So, did Longwood kill the cleaner?" Catherine asked.

"We're not sure yet, but we don't think so. Longwood says Bradshaw hired someone, at the suggestion of one of the inmates, to rob the guy."

"Of course, this is a crucial point for Longwood—it could mean the death penalty if he did the hiring," George said. "We're still working that angle."

"Anyway, that was one thing we had right—it was a robbery gone bad," Manny said. Just then Peaches topped the stairs. Looking around, she saw her master; she went to him and laid down at his feet, placing her chin on his shoe. "The guy after the keys killed the cleaner," Manny said, stroking the silky head of his companion. "He took the keys, his watch, and emptied his pockets to make it look like a robbery. He hid the body, and then found his way, with a stop at Ben's office, to Brenda's computer lab where he planted the devices."

"We did sweep all your offices," Dani said, "but we didn't find any other bugs."

"So your theory that the robber got the keypad code from my desk is right?" Sitwell asked.

"Yes, although Longwood didn't know about the keypad, the robber was clever enough to figure it out. Payoff money is a strong motivator, shall we say."

"Miss Catherine?"

Startled, by the sudden voice through the intercom, everyone looked over into the empty space of the room.

Catherine laughed. "Well, I think we should leave our ghost story for now. Dinner must be ready, so let's go down or Lucy will be very upset after all the cooking she's done. We can continue this tale with our dinner wine."

Setting their empty cocktail glasses on the blueprint counter, everyone trooped down the stairs. Manny and Catherine led the parade. He took her arm as she held tight to the railing. Brenda and Fred brought up the rear.

"Brenda you look stunning tonight," Fred said, enfolding her in his arms and giving her a sweet kiss, then holding her tight for an instant before letting her go.

"Come on, detective," Brenda whispered in his ear, "let's catch up with the others before they send Dani back up after us."

Conversation was lively as Wendy made the rounds pouring the wine—no one deferred. Catherine indicated a half a glass would be nice for her.

Russell stood to propose a toast. "Here's to a most incredible group of people. I thank you all for your loyalty and diligence in saving Stone & Associates, and in saving me."

"Here here," Fatigate said, as they all raised their glasses.

Russell didn't sit down. Instead he softly tapped his crystal wine goblet. Everyone looked back at him, quizzical expressions on their faces, watching him walk to the opposite end of the table. "I have an announcement to make, a very pleasant announcement I might add. As of last Friday, the lady sitting at the head of this lovely table accepted and signed the documents to become a full partner in Stone & Associates."

Several took in a breath of surprise. All were wide eyed, and in unison stood, raising their wine glasses in a salute to Catherine. Applause broke out. Words of congratulations, well deserved, and bravo were heard.

Catherine rose, flushed, beaming, and nodded to her friends and colleagues. "Thank you, all, and especially you, Russell." They gave each other a gentle hug as Catherine whispered, "Thank you," in his ear. "Now, please help yourselves to the buffet table. I'm not sure what all is there as Lucy has added a couple of her specialties."

In short order, plates were filled and the guests returned to their seats, ready to enjoy the turkey, ham, and duck as well as the accompanying dishes.

"Brenda, you must be relieved to have this behind you," Dani said to her dinner partner.

"You bet I am. As you know, I still have to appear at an inquest, but Fred doesn't think I'll have any problems. At Russell's insistence the computer lab was moved to the first floor, to a room in the middle of the building. Now I'm performing all the backups, security functions, and system manager responsibilities from my office computer over the network. I only go to the lab occasionally, but it's still a mushroom factory," Brenda said, laughing. "Sorry, Russell, but that's how a room feels with no windows."

"Russell, has Victoria Standish been bothering you anymore?" George asked.

"No, we haven't heard a peep out of her lately," Russell replied. "I hope her lack of activity isn't just a temporary respite. Chuck, you haven't seen her poking around have you?"

"No, and it's a good thing, too" Sanchez said. "I'm afraid I'd give her a piece of my mind."

"She's a piece of work, that's for sure," George interjected.

"Manny, please finish your story about Longwood," Brenda said. "He seems to have done most of the dirty work for Bradshaw."

"Yes, he was certainly a busy bee, traveling all over Europe, sending you and Russell messages. He also made a stop in Cancun. Bradshaw had stashed two-million dollars in a bank account there long before he was arrested for the murder of Russell's wife," Manny said with sadness in his voice and looking at Russell.

"Bradshaw told Longwood about the money and how to access it," Manny continued. "They used this money to fund their cyber crime. He made a stop in Cancun, to replenish his bank account before returning to Daytona Beach. Longwood made a fatal error at the end when he tried to transfer ten-million dollars from Stone & Associates bank account from the House of Beads Cyber Café. Because of Brenda's trap, we were able to respond immediately, catching him in the act."

"That was some trap you set up, my friend," Dani said, flashing a smile at Brenda.

"Of course," Manny continued, "all hell broke loose when Bradshaw pulled his escape. We found out from Balfor that Longwood had bribed the guard with $5,000 if he would facilitate Bradshaw's flight to freedom. The poor sucker didn't know the devil he was dealing with. The intention all along was to kill him, so he couldn't squeal later. You all know the rest that happened in the computer lab."

Russell stood and faced Brenda, the others followed his lead. "Brenda, when you and I first met, you told me that Homeland Security had hired you as a *rookie* agent. I think everyone will agree that you have now earned your stripes." Raising his glass, he said, "To Brenda. You are one tough, courageous lady. I'm glad you're on our side."

One by one, the friends circled the table, giving Brenda a hug. In turn, Fred gave her a discreet peck on the cheek as he looked lovingly into her eyes.

Epilogue

—•••—

Four weeks later

IT WAS 2:12 AM, only six minutes since the last time Catherine looked at the clock. Timing her contractions, they had increased to five or six minutes apart and seemed to be coming stronger. Excitement that her baby was on its way, yet apprehensive at what the next few hours held for her, she got out of bed and headed to Lucy's room across the hall.

"Lucy, it's Catherine," she said, knocking softly.

Lucy opened her door. "Miss Catherine, is everything all right?"

"I think it's time, Lucy. I've called the doctor, and his service said to go on to the hospital. They're calling him to meet me there. Will you get Brenda up?"

"Oh, Miss Catherine, this is so exciting. Yes, I'll get Brenda. You get dressed but don't go down those stairs until we're by your side. We don't want anything to happen to you or that precious lad you're carrying."

Catherine went back to her room to dress, and to take one last inventory of the small overnight case she had packed a few weeks ago. "Little Stephen, I hope you like your new nightshirt. It may be too small, but if you're a big guy, mommy will get you another one. My sweet boy, I can't wait to hold you." Catherine closed the case as she heard Lucy hustle down the stairs calling softly to Brenda.

Brenda heard Lucy calling which meant only one thing— Catherine was in labor. She met Lucy at the door before she could knock.

"Lucy, is it time?" Brenda asked.

"Yes. Miss Catherine is dressing. I told her not to budge down the stairs until we came for her."

"Good. I'll bring the car around to the front door. I'll be with you in a jiffy. Oh, Lucy, isn't this exciting?" Brenda said, giving Lucy a quick hug.

Leaving the car at the front door, Brenda hurried back inside to help Catherine down the stairs. Lucy took the suitcase and preceded the two, but only by a few stairs in case Catherine stumbled.

Before she knew it, Catherine was in the car on her way to meet her son.

"How are you feeling, kiddo?" Brenda asked. "Can you time the contractions? God, I'm getting nervous and excited at the same time. Thank heaven I went to that Lamaze class with you. I'm going to have to do some deep breathing myself once we get in your birthing room. Wow, I just said birthing room."

"Brenda, the contractions are getting a little harder. Are we almost there?" Catherine asked, squeezing Lucy's hand.

"We're here, Catherine. Lucy you stay with her, I'll run in and get an orderly and a wheelchair."

Brenda returned as promised. The orderly helped Catherine into the wheelchair and headed into the hospital.

"Lucy, here, take her suitcase and go with her. I'll park the car and will be right up," Brenda said, handing the case to Lucy who followed behind the orderly.

By the time Brenda joined Catherine in the birthing room, Dr. Colton was already assessing her progress.

"I think this little guy is anxious to get into this world, Catherine. As we discussed, the anesthesiologist will give you an epidural which will ease your discomfort considerably. You're dilating very quickly."

— ••• —

When asked later, Catherine couldn't remember too much about what happened. After the epidural the birth happened very fast. She remembered Brenda and Lucy on either side of her, holding her hand, as the doctor requested her to push and then to relax. She could faintly remember hearing herself crying out in pain as she pushed with all of her might.

But the one moment she remembered most was hearing little Stephen let out a wail as he came forth into his new world. Everyone was crying with joy as the doctor laid the little bundle in his mother's arms. Someone must have called Manny, because he was beside her bed along with Brenda and Lucy. He unashamedly let the tears roll down his cheeks.

Catherine asked Brenda to dial the telephone number she had given her days before.

"Hello, Meri. It's Catherine. Your grandson is here, and he's perfect...I'll call you when we get home...I love you, too."

Catherine's eyes, filled with tears of joy, looked into Brenda's teary face. She handed the phone back to Brenda and whispered, "Thank you."

Cradling her baby boy, Catherine said, gazing down at the precious bundle, "Little Stephen, let me present you to your new family. Brenda, Lucy, Manny—I'd like you to meet my son, Stephen Hutchinson Hainsworth."

The End

REVIEW REQUEST

Dear reader, if you have the time, it would mean a lot to me if you wrote a review, your honest appraisal. What did you like most? It's super easy. Go to Amazon. Log in. Search: <u>Mary Jane Forbes Checkmate.</u> Thank you!

Identity Theft, Terrorists on the Prowl
Book four – *House of Beads Mystery Series*

He's presumed dead. She's lost the last thing she has from their love. Infiltrating a terrorist ring will either bring them together or get him killed...

Stephen Hutchinson isn't sure he'll ever recover. After all, the gunshot wounds and his faked death took him away from the love of his life. When his partner tells him Catherine has moved on, Stephen throws himself into an undercover operation to stop a terrorist network. Little does he know that his case and his love are destined to collide...

New mother Catherine Hainsworth will never forget the father of her child. But as she focuses on raising Stephen Jr. and growing her business, she has no idea her son has been targeted. With Catherine's son kidnapped, the safety of her child may depend on the love she never gave up on.

In a race to take down the terrorists, Stephen has one chance to reunite his family before a modern-day menace destroys their only shot at happiness.

Identity Theft is the fourth standalone book and the thrilling conclusion to the House of Beads romantic suspense series. If you like action-packed plots, high-tech mysteries, and heart-wrenching romance, then you'll love Mary Jane Forbes' riveting novel.

Buy *Identity Theft* to go undercover for love today!

Books by Mary Jane Forbes

FICTION

Bradley Farm Series
Bradley Farm, Sadie, Finn
Jeli, Marshall, Georgie

Twists of Fate Series
The Fisherman, a love story
The Witness, living a lie
Twists of Fate, daring to dream

Murder by Design, Series:
Murder by Design
Labeled in Seattle
Choices, And the Courage to Risk

Elizabeth Stitchway, PI, Series
The Mailbox, Black Magic,
The Painter, Twister

House of Beads Mystery Series
Murder in the House of Beads
Intercept, Checkmate
Identity Theft

Novels
The Baby Quilt ... a mystery!
The Message...Call Me!

Short Stories
Once Upon a Christmas Eve, a Romantic Fairy Tale
The Christmas Angel and the Magic Holiday Tree

Visit: www.MaryJaneForbes.com

www.ingramcontent.com/pod-product-compliance
Lightning Source LLC
Chambersburg PA
CBHW070824120626
46556CB00002B/648